PRAISE FOR ELIZABETH SPENCER'S
JACK OF DIAMONDS

"A writer well worth reading and rereading. Few books of short fiction measure up to this one, which may be the best of the season."
— *The Washington Post Book World*

"High on that list of the best southern writers is the name of Elizabeth Spencer."
— *Newsday*

"Her stories brim over with substance and detail, with a vernacular so intimate you can't help thinking she grew up next door to her characters."
— *The Boston Sunday Globe*

"Of the five outstanding stories in this collection by a master of the genre, at least three qualify as classics. All are beautifully honed, animated by distinctive characters and deeply expressive."
— *Publishers Weekly*

"Stories by a real artist who possesses wisdom, wit, and the sharp edge of biting intelligence that is so rare and so undercelebrated."
— Robb Forman Dew, *USA Today*

"Dazzling, highly original, memorable"
— Walker Percy

"A master storyteller . . . her unerring imagination, eye for detail, and social irony remain as strong as ever."
— *San Francisco Chronicle*

"Ms. Spencer has a master's touch for rendering the spirit of the setting. . . . This quality gives her stories much greater depth than is commonly found in contemporary short fiction; every one of them is substantial enough to make up an entire novel."
— *The New York Times Book Review*

"Spencer writes prose so smooth you could pour it on pancakes."
— *St. Petersburg Times*

"Spencer is . . . intensely [illegible] he lies they live and the truths they [illegible] crafted and honest."
— *Time*

The author wishes to thank the Rockefeller Foundation for their invitation to the Villa Serbelloni, Bellagio, Italy, where several of these stories were either written or commenced.

CONTEMPORARY AMERICAN FICTION

JACK OF DIAMONDS

Elizabeth Spencer is the author of numerous short-story collections and highly praised novels, including *Fire in the Morning* and *The Light in the Piazza*. She is the recipient of many prizes, including the Rosenthal Award of the American Academy of Arts and Letters, a Guggenheim Fellowship, and the Award of Merit Medal for the Short Story, given by the American Academy of Arts and Letters. She is a member of the American Institute of Arts and Letters. Three of the stories in this collection have been included in editions of the *O. Henry Prize Stories*, and a fourth has appeared in *The Pushcart Prize: Best of the Small Presses*. Currently at work on a new novel, Ms. Spencer lives in Chapel Hill, North Carolina, with her husband.

For Louis and Eva Rubin
and for Max Steele

JACK OF DIAMONDS

AND OTHER STORIES BY

ELIZABETH SPENCER

PENGUIN BOOKS

PENGUIN BOOKS
Published by the Penguin Group
Viking Penguin, a division of Penguin Books USA Inc.,
40 West 23rd Street, New York, New York 10010, U.S.A.
Penguin Books Ltd, 27 Wrights Lane,
London W8 5TZ, England
Penguin Books Australia Ltd, Ringwood,
Victoria, Australia
Penguin Books Canada Ltd, 2801 John Street,
Markham, Ontario, Canada L3R 1B4
Penguin Books (N.Z.) Ltd, 182–190 Wairau Road,
Auckland 10, New Zealand

Penguin Books Ltd, Registered Offices:
Harmondsworth, Middlesex, England

First published in the United States of America
by Viking Penguin, a division of
Penguin Books USA Inc. 1988
Published in Penguin Books 1989

1 3 5 7 9 10 8 6 4 2

"Jean-Pierre" first appeared in *The New Yorker;* "The Cousins" and "The Business Venture" in *The Southern Review;* "Jack of Diamonds" in *The Kenyon Review;* and "The Skater" in *North American Review.*

LIBRARY OF CONGRESS CATALOGING IN PUBLICATION DATA
Spencer, Elizabeth.
Jack of diamonds and other stories/ by Elizabeth Spencer.
p. cm. — (Contemporary American fiction).
Originally published: New York, N.Y., U.S.A.: Viking, 1988.
Contents: Jean-Pierre — The cousins — Jack of diamonds — The business venture — The skater.
ISBN 0 14 01.2252 4
I. Title. II. Series.
[PS3537.P4454J33 1989]
813'.54—dc19 89-2928

Printed in the United States of America
Set in Garamond No. 3

CONTENTS

JEAN-PIERRE

"My father was a car salesman out in N.D.G.," Callie told Monsieur Courtois; then, recognizing that his English was poor, she tried out her French. *"Mon père a vendu des autos à Notre-Dame-de-Grâce."*

"He died, then?"

"Oh, no, he and his wife left Montreal. They moved to California about a year ago—in 1962. *Maintenant ils demeurent—*"

"I know," he cut her off. "And you stayed."

"My sister's here."

"Votre soeur est ici," he said, perversely switching to French. *"Vous habitez chez elle?"*

"Je suis seule."

"Vous êtes seule," he repeated, and a while later said, *"Pourquoi?"*

But by then she had forgotten the first part, and, being a little wary of him, uncertain, she said, *"Comment?"*

"I said why do you live alone?"

"My sister is married, so . . ."

"You work?"

"Yes, I work."

He did not seem interested enough to ask her where. The Fletchers, who had asked her along to help entertain their friend, came back from across the street; they had gone to see when the movie would start. Jean-Pierre Courtois, the friend (he was actually a business prospect), ordered another round of drinks.

After the movie, they all went to have pizza. Callie watched Monsieur Courtois while he was too intent on eating to look up and find her watching. He was dark, almost swart, with a fleshy face that could, she guessed, go sullen rather easily; his full, smooth mouth stirred with annoyance when he could not part the cheese strings from the pizza without winding them off onto his fork. He stuffed in mouthfuls that were too large, and chewed with first one cheek full, then the other. But his clothes were neat, his tie quiet, and the only thing that really set him off from the English-speaking Fletchers was the slight gleam of artificial gloss on his thick hair, and the gold he wore—cuff links, ring, and tie clip, all very bright. Callie's stepmother, with her querulous voice, would have called him "Mister" Courtois, not "Monsieur," and said that he looked cheap, dismissing him for good and all. O.K., thought Callie, he looks cheap. I've done my duty to Kay and Bob Fletcher. I'll never see him again.

After the movie and the pizza, and after a last drink at the Fletchers' apartment out on Côte-des-Neiges, he drove her home. She lived near Sherbrooke on Saint-Marc, in an old building, ground floor, with a yard behind it. In the arch of the doorway, he stopped her. "You watched me. *Tout le temps.* Why?"

She shook her head, though he was right; she hadn't wondered why. He stepped her into the corner by the door, pressed against the whole of her, and kissed her. *"C'est ça que tu veux?"* he said roughly.

She never answered. She shook so she could hardly get the key into the lock; by the time she did, he was in the car and about to start it, which she turned back to watch him do. He drove off without a glance. Getting angry as she closed the door, she finally began to speak aloud to herself. "I'm too young for him. I can't speak his damn language. He knows all that." She whammed her bag down on the apartment table. The kiss had been an act of contempt, she thought; she had got that out of it. The French did not like English-speaking people. They did not take them out. He had been contemptuous of the Fletchers' choice for him; Bob's chance of selling him any insurance was gone. They should have asked a French girl for the evening.

Contempt, again, was what she heard in his voice when he phoned her a week later, saying his name so fast she couldn't think who he might be, and she said it was the wrong number, until he told her more clearly. Why did she agree to meet him? She didn't know; she wished she hadn't.

He sat across from her, in a booth in a place that advertised steak from Texas steers, and he looked at her—this time it was she who was watched while eating—and smoked, and asked her questions. Sometimes he was silent. "I like your hair," he told her suddenly. She got angry again, and couldn't eat another bite.

Her hair was pale, fine, and straight. It hung down evenly on either side, and was a little longer in the back, where it dipped down into a V. He must be thirty years old, she thought, and probably married. She did not even try to talk to him. She was still so young, scarcely turned twenty, and given to quietness. Since her mother's death she had endured a bitter family life, prone to fights and festering. She had studied French to get the voices out of her head.

But then she began to think of what the French went through here, treated as inferior by the English, called names they resented (she didn't blame them); they preferred a life unmarred by violating eyes and scarring comments—such regard, such words as her stepmother had gone in for. So, as she remembered this, her humor improved and she said kindly, *"Merci."*

"What?"

"I said thank you. For dinner. For saying you liked my hair."

"Bienvenue," he answered. Bad French, she knew, but she let it go.

It was her hair he touched at the door, and this time he came inside to kiss her. Departing, his car made its accustomed skidding noise at the corner. The scene just past was a still-spinning disk, and she clung dizzily to its center, thinking, I've never got into things like this before.

But then maybe it had to happen sometime, with somebody. And maybe, she thought, it was why she'd stayed on in Montreal alone rather than going to California, why she'd moved out of her sister's house and asked her not to tell their father, for fear of starting all sorts of family worrying and suspicions—those quarrels now grown silent.

That was in May. In June, she married him.

Her sister had her out to Notre-Dame-de-Grâce when she heard the plan, and sat her down at the kitchen table with coffee in a ceramic mug covered with yellow daisies. "You can't do this, Callie. He's one of those awful Quebec people. They left France so long ago nobody there knows they exist. We met somebody from Paris the other day who still couldn't understand a word of their French after two weeks here. You'll wind up with fifteen brats and not even good French. Why didn't you just get rid of him?"

"You know somehow," said Callie, "when someone is permanent in your life. You can marry them or not marry them; they're always there just the same."

"That's the most childish thing I ever heard of," her sister said. "Unless you've got in trouble and won't tell me."

Her sister's name was Beatrice, but she cultivated an English tone and liked people to call her Bea. To save Callie from defending herself against the charge of childishness—or not defending herself—the phone rang. It was Bart, her brother-in-law, wanting to speak to her.

"I knew Bea was going to talk to you today, but I don't know if she'll tell you what I said. In my opinion, I think you don't believe any of us loves you, Callie. Well, whatever you think, that's not true. We do love you."

"Thank you," she said.

"Will you just remember that one thing? We love you."

She said she would remember.

"And then," said Bea when Callie returned to the table, "there's your social life, for instance. What kind of husband image is he going to be? Bart and I make an impression, I know that. Even our names go together—you have to think of everything. But 'Jean-Pierre and Callie,' how does that sound?"

"Terrible," said Callie.

"And then the financial side. At least, you must have talked it over."

"He makes a good living. He told me so."

"He owns property—"

"He owns two apartment houses," said Callie, though she knew Bea had informed herself of that already, just by the way she stopped. "They're out in East Montreal."

"Have you seen them?"

"No, have you?"

"Don't be ridiculous," said Bea. "Of course not. Why would I go there? Nobody lives over there but—oh, you know, plumbers." She always doubted whether Callie ate enough, and whacked off a wedge of coffee cake for her now.

"They must exist," said Callie, "because Bob Fletcher wanted to sell him insurance for them."

"What did Bart want?" asked Bea.

"He said he thought I thought you didn't love me."

"That's ridiculous," said Bea. "Why do you think I wanted to talk to you?"

"I don't know," said Callie.

"You'll never see his money," said Bea. "I'm certain of that."

"I guess he'll buy the groceries," said Callie, getting stubborn. She had not, to tell the truth, discussed finances. She had found out the simplest way—by going there when invited—that his apartment was in midtown, and that he could afford anything he wanted; he didn't have to think twice.

To Callie, the real question was not why she wanted to marry Jean-Pierre, with whom she felt she belonged, but why he wanted to marry her—this English-speaking girl, so much younger, with nothing to offer him. Because he liked her, he said. His first wife had died. The family had blamed him. He brought the confidence out reluctantly, like information it was dangerous to share. It seemed he had got a bad name in the French community—the strict side of it. He could move into other French circles, but they would find out eventually. Besides, since he was Catholic, Callie was never sure that he thought he was really marrying her, in the final, true sense, at all. They had a ceremony in the office of a French Protestant church, down in the shadow of the Pont Jacques-Cartier. There were some dusty green textbooks on theology on glass-fronted shelves; a desk, a lectern, and a rug worn colorless. The witnesses were Jean-Pierre's uncle and Callie's former landlady, who left soon after—she had an appointment. Bea and Bart were away, she supposed because they disapproved. They had invited her and Jean-Pierre to dinner at the Beaver Club before they left, and given them a Waterford fruit bowl and a check. But their absence stung her, even though the excuse was plausible; Bart had an interview for a high position in a Cincinnati brokerage firm, and it could not be postponed.

Jean-Pierre gave a wedding luncheon for some of his friends, relatives, and business connections and their wives, girlfriends, and mistresses. One even brought along a cousin of his own. Jean-Pierre smoked a lot and paid Callie little notice. "Died of blood poisoning in the hospital," she overheard him saying at one point. "She got it there. In the hospital. Some doctor her family knew. Why blame me? I wasn't with her every hour, every minute. I had to keep food on the table. What they said was 'But did you have to be in Quebec City?' 'I was where I had to be,' I said, 'even if it was Miami, Florida.' "

He went on in French to another man: "Stay out of hospitals—the best thing is take care of yourself. . . . Her mother never talked to me again. 'Look, Madame,' I told her, 'you lost your daughter, but me, I lost my wife. Which is worse?' 'She lived with me all those years,' she says. 'That's a stupid question.' 'O.K.,' I told her, 'but you have to admit it's a stupid idea to think I killed her.' 'Where were you when she died?'—she must have said that a hundred times. If she were here right now, she'd be saying that—'Where were you when my daughter died?' My God, those women . . . Big, strong . . . She'd cry; O.K., you'd expect that, but every tear so fat and swollen! That's enough. Let's drop it."

From across the table, a friend, perhaps another uncle, raised a champagne glass and clinked it with Jean-Pierre's. He lit a cigar. They had yet to drink to her. In fact, they never did, though in parting they all kissed her hand. *"Bonne chance,"* they kept saying. *"Merci,"* she said. They assumed she knew no French. Yet she understood them well enough. Alone with Jean-Pierre, she spoke to him in his language.

They drove over the border to Burlington for the weekend, ate at a good restaurant, went to the Holiday Inn, and everything was the same as ever. For some reason, they cared about each other. He said that it would be *une union heureuse et éternelle*—she would see.

Jean-Pierre had thick dark hair, darker than most of his

friends', and gray eyes nearly as dark as coal. He looked almost Spanish, she told him once or twice. He said she didn't know what she was talking about; he was altogether French; his family had come over in *mille six cent quatre-vingt trois*, among the first settlers.

"I'm sorry your wife died like that," Callie ventured the first evening. "I didn't know it was like that."

"Why mention it?" Jean-Pierre asked.

All the second day he was laughing and gay. He told her funny stories, one after another. She ate a lot for lunch and dinner, and felt happier than she ever had before. I did the right thing, she thought. Nobody would know that but me. The next day, driving back to Montreal, something went a little wrong with the car—the gas line clogged—and Jean-Pierre was unhappy and silent all the way to the Champlain Bridge.

Jean-Pierre took her over to East Montreal to see his two properties: dark brick buildings, of forty-five apartments each, he said, with doorways made of yellow stained oak set with mottled glass, and painted in slanting gold letters: "Les Tuileries," "Le Trianon." It was a close humid day, misting rain, and narrow iron balconies along the sides of the buildings were crammed like rush-hour buses with sweating people in shorts, T-shirts, and sandals. Smoke rose from a barbecue. The windows all seemed dull. Somebody looked over a balcony railing and noticed Jean-Pierre and threw something down—maybe just an empty carton. Another person yelled at them. "Would you like to go inside?" he asked her. "*Non, merci*," said Callie, and that night she had a dream of the buildings, windows crowded with painted, shouting faces, the people all fat and too big for the small rooms behind them, all sweating and smoke-stained and complaining of noise.

What did she know about it? If she tried to ask too much he would brood—a brooding so deep and thorough that his eyes seemed to peer beautifully into her soul's depth. A mystery so deep couldn't be just about business. Perhaps it was his dead wife haunting him; perhaps he felt guilty about her. Had he known some other woman, who was unkind to him? Was he in debt? Had a friend betrayed him? Was he bored with Callie and regretting that he had married her? She asked him. *"Mais non, ma p'tite . . . pourquoi tu parles comme ça?"*

They moved from his old apartment into a larger place and furnished it through a cousin of Jean-Pierre's—a dealer in Saint-Laurent—who had given them a discount price. Most of the pieces were imitation Danish modern, but the wood was real.

In early June, when they had been married for nearly a year, Jean-Pierre disappeared.

She had come in from grocery shopping and found a note on the dining table, weighted down with the Waterford bowl: "I will be gone for a while, *c'est nécessaire.* There is money in the bank, two thousand." After a week she thought about notifying the police, but something put her off that. She thought of calling the building superintendent of Les Tuileries and Le Trianon. She was afraid of actually knowing. He might be in some sort of trouble. But maybe it wasn't his fault. Phone calls came in French for Jean-Pierre. *"Il est hors de la ville,"* she said. *"C'est impossible . . . Je ne sais pas . . . Je n'ai aucune idée."*

Then she had a call from Bob Fletcher. "Excuse me, Callie," he said, "but I heard Courtois is about to sell those apartments on Rue Rachel."

"I don't know about his business," said Callie.

"We insured them, you know. He was having some trouble getting coverage—it wasn't clear if they were residential or offices. We wanted the account, at first. I was trying to expand to the French. That first evening, remember? Sure you do. Later I pulled off from it. I'd have dropped it, but Bart insisted. Bart was worried because he thought you might be getting hooked up with the wrong guy. Who's to say? Anyway, I went ahead with it. You're getting on O.K., I hope."

'He isn't here," said Callie. "I'll tell him. I'm fine."

When she hung up, the phone rang again, and a woman's voice asked in French for Jean-Pierre. It was something to do with money from Trois-Rivières which was expected in some other town, in Rimouski, and Callie thought she heard the words "*son fils*." (His son? Impossible! But maybe it wasn't.)

"Find him yourself!" she said in English. This provoked a long eruption, but she couldn't make out the words and she began to cry. That was wrong—the wrong thing to do.

The weather was hot. From the apartment windows she often looked down on the area in back of a shabby house—one of a row of old houses that, on the street side, had steep stairs up to the front doors, each topped by an ornate second-floor balcony with a triangular roof, no two quite alike. Behind this house there was a small garden with a lounge chair, where a woman sunned herself on weekends. Callie had bought a new bathing suit and some white sandals she especially liked. Having no place now to wear either, she went one twilight and talked to the woman in the house, asking if she could use the chair on weekday afternoons.

"You can keep it from being stolen," the woman said. "I had one stolen last year, and now I've chained this one to the fence. But I think somebody is going to take it anyway." And she gave Callie the key to the back gate.

So for a week Callie sunned in the chair, latching and unlatching the new sandals and soaking the sun into her fair skin. A cat, its white fur stippled in silky gray, marched back and forth on the back steps from time to time. It also climbed the board fence between that yard and the next, and, finding a post and a wooden ledge to balance on, curled tail around feet and sat regarding her. She made some contact with the steady slate-blue gaze; a current ran from the sun to her, from the cat to her, from her to the cat. She had felt alone and anxious, numb and half dead, but now there was a joining, a new sense of life. When she looked up, she expected to see herself on the narrow back balcony of her apartment, looking down. The weather held. On the third day, when she went inside the cat followed her.

All absences are mysterious. Whether the absence is understood or not, the absent person is, somehow, not really gone. "Not gone," Callie wrote down on her grocery list. Not being physically present, his thoughts became all-important. They filled the sky; they overweighed the world. But what were they? "Thinks of me," she wrote next, then added, "But what?" Sometimes she could hear him talking, clearly, in her head, but to someone else: "*J'ai un mal de tête effrayant.*" . . . "*Les gens sont fous.*" . . . "*Elle est trop jeune . . . une enfant . . . presque.*"

To stop these conversations she took several sleeping pills—over-the-counter things that did very little good. All weekend, the cat slept on the foot of the bed and purred. That Monday she had to acknowledge that the money had shrunk, that bills, bills, bills kept coming in, that the rent was due. She went to a library out in N.D.G. where she had worked before she married—what seemed an age ago.

In the spacious, book-scented room, its windows open on a warm, overcast day, Mrs. Gentian was still behind the desk. She gave Callie a toothy, affectionate smile. She was a hurrying, eager soul, anxious for things to run right and for people to be happy. She believed that books increased the happiness of the human race. She imagined that Callie had come back because she liked her, and missed her, and wanted to say hello. Callie knew this and hated to disappoint her, but she had to.

"Can I help out with anything during the summer, Mrs. Gentian? I just need to make some extra money."

"Well, my dear, I don't know. . . . Somebody told me you got married."

"I did. He's away right now. For the summer."

"Tell me. Is he English or what?"

"French—Quebec French."

"Well . . . they're different," said Mrs. Gentian, and she looked away, resettling her glasses. She said that Callie could come in part-time, and gave her the record collection to handle. But it took very little time to sort and rearrange and recatalogue them, and check them in and out for the few habitués who wanted to go sit at a record player in a windowless cubicle on a green summer day, so Callie was mainly at Mrs. Gentian's beck and call for minor errands and duties. And sometimes she just sat and read.

It was poetry she kept looking at now. She'd tried to talk about poetry to Jean-Pierre; he had mentioned Saint-Denys Garneau, whom he'd heard of but never read, and Mallarmé, whom he'd studied in school but could not remember.

Callie sat and read Emily Dickinson. She read it line for line. A whole book lay before her, and she thought it might just last all summer; poetry went much more slowly than a novel. She learned that nature was marvelous but cruel, that death was inexorable, that to lose your love was another sort of death, that God was somebody whom, if you had any sense at all, you had to argue with. Montreal was muggy, overcast, and dirty that summer. The trees in the residential streets looked cool and full, but downtown near her own apartment, along Sainte-Catherine, vomit dried in various shades of green all day outside the *tavernes,* and all dogs seemed afflicted with diarrhea. She went back and forth to N.D.G. on the bus. Like filling a bucket in a mountain lake, she tried to fill her mind with the poems of Emily Dickinson and the concerned kindness of Mrs. Gentian, who had sensed that something was wrong and had quit asking her about her husband.

But the comfort leaked away during the night, and every dawn she woke in a dry-tongued fright, wondering, What can I do? Whom can I go to? Sooner or later she would have to tell someone. The concierge's wife kept asking, "*Quand est-ce qu'il revient?* Is he gone forever?" and Callie kept saying, "Next week, I think," and gave her a check for the rent.

My life closed twice before its close.

She wasn't going so far yet as to say she was dying. It was just that, except for the cat, the lounge chair, and the sandals, she felt alone. If she told Mrs. Gentian, she would have sympathy, but the feeling would not end. If she called Bea and Bart in Cincinnati, Bea would say I told you so, you ought to have had more sense. Bart would worry, and call Bob Fletcher, or maybe fly in, and they would start managing things. When the English managed things, who cared about the French? She knew that much. She wrote to her father and stepmother in California that everything was fine. The slanting script of her letter looked too small for the page, so she drew happy little climbing vines up either side to frame it. At the table in the library, with moist air leaking some water against the windows ("spotting," the English called it; "*maussade,*" said the French), she thought about nature in New England, perhaps still full of tall elms—the elms that were sick and dying in Montreal, some already chopped down and hauled away. Full, too, of hummingbirds, and berry bushes growing up the slopes of hills, of robins dining on fat worms, of swarms of butterflies dancing in inexhaustible sunlight. Well, she guessed the Laurentians were nice, too—she could take a bus up there some Sunday and see things like that; it was just that nobody had written about them that way, nobody she knew of. And there was all this thing about life, love, hurting, that wound through everything this woman was thinking about or looking at.

> *My reason, life,*
> *I had not had, but for yourself.*
> *'Twere better charity*
> *To leave me in the atom's tomb.*

"What's 'the atom's tomb'?" she suddenly asked the young man across from her at the library table. He had come there for four days in a row, had sat facing her each time, and read, after parking a baby in a stroller at his side. The baby usually slept; the young man read magazines. He had uncontrollably curly dark hair, shabbily cut, and gnawed fingernails, and he wore a short-sleeved beige shirt and no tie. Why did he always sit opposite her? All the other tables were empty. Might as well ask why the cat had put its head up over the fence.

"You're still reading those same poems," he said.

"They're about New England," she said.

"I read different things," he said.

"Different how?"

"I try to vary my reading."

She did not reply. She got up to help Mrs. Gentian sort through some new periodicals and put them on the racks, replacing the older ones, which she brought in a stack to the desk for filing. She was wearing the sandals, a wraparound skirt, and a faded coral blouse. She felt the young man watching the sandals. He was like someone approaching a door.

When she returned to the table, he asked, "Why do you like New England?"

"Because of what I'm reading about it," she said, and laughed, the answer having led him in a circle, as she knew it would.

He did not smile. " 'The atom's tomb' would be what you were still in if you'd never become human or been born, I guess. I think I read that, too, once."

She observed him with more tolerance. He looked intelligent in a harried way; she thought he was probably Jewish. "Why do you bring that baby every day?"

"Where else would I leave her?" he asked.

"I don't know," she said, and began to read again, having (all roads led to Rome) come close to the subject of wives and husbands.

"My wife works," he pursued anyway. He was the kind of library reader who sat down on his backbone instead of on his hips, legs stretched out (sidewise, to miss her own), feet crossed at the ankles, elbows spread on the tabletop to their farthest reach, his face nearly dipping into the book. He was arranged like a geometrical design. He seemed to be speaking to her through a magnified web of the print he was just reading from. "I'm out of a job. I got fired. My wife works. I have to mind the baby."

I measure every grief I meet
With analytic eyes;
I wonder if it weighs like mine,
Or has an easier size.

"Are you scared?" she asked him. She hadn't meant to say that.

"Of course," he said breathlessly, and the sense of contact made her dizzy.

"The brain is just the weight of God," Callie read. What on earth did that mean?

"This morning," he said, "I fell over the stroller on my way for the mail. I knew it was there, but I fell over it."

"Oh," she said, and remembered a nightmare she had had the night before—Jean-Pierre driving by on Sherbrooke Street and laughing at her while the light changed. Somebody she'd met once, somebody she'd married in a dream he hadn't had.

"I've watched you every day," the young man said. "Something's the matter with you, too. Nobody reads poetry the way you've been doing unless something's the matter."

She didn't answer—any more than if he had addressed the white cat. Thinking of the cat, she put out her tongue's tip and then drew it in again. Thus would the cat have done, adjusting one paw. Finally she said, in a careful way, not wishing to add to troubles by the weight of a feather, "What's that matter to you?"

"I don't know," he said, after considering the question. "I have this feeling that something's happening to both of us, that we're having the same sort of struggle about whatever it is. I'm worried, you're worried. I'm scared, you're scared."

"Then maybe," she suggested, "we'd do better to be around somebody who didn't feel that way."

"That may be true," he replied. "But I wonder if we wouldn't be better able to get along with a likeness than a difference, at this point. I mean, if you're sinking in the ocean, you need somebody to pull you out. But if you're falling through space, a companion in flight is about the best you can hope for."

"I don't know which it is," she said, and went back to her book.

The Carriage held but just Ourselves
And Immortality.

That was company of another kind. Closing the book, she got up to help Mrs. Gentian at the desk. The young man was watching her as she moved. He was watching her sandals walking. The cat, she recalled, watched in a different way, yet this regard, too, cut through the stifling web of her anxiety.

In August, the library closed, and she and the young man, whose name was Simon Weiss, drove down to New England for the day in a car he had borrowed from his uncle Stan. It was a fine, clear, sky-blue, fresh summer day.

They went south to Swanton, in Vermont, then turned east into beautiful farm country over little-known roads that led through green-and-white villages. Uncle Stan's car was a blue Volkswagen with a tick in its noisy motor. The fenders were splotched with maroon paint to cover the rust.

"There's a farm down a road near here," said Simon. "My mother knew a lady who lived there. She rented a room from her for a while once, when she was getting over an operation. I can't think of her name. It's a pretty place. You'll like it. We'll get some food and go there." He stopped at a grocery in the next town. He said the farm was five miles from there, but it seemed more like ten.

Later, all she remembered of the farm was the quarry, out of use, deserted, at the end of a small road that ran beside the farmhouse. At the house they stood and called, then knocked, but no one answered. There wasn't even a dog. Callie thought someone was inside just the same.

In the quarry, they split up the food from the grocery sack and ate it—cheese and crackers, salami, ham, and bread, a box of cakes, Cokes, and beer. The sun was hot. The rocks were flat from having had other rocks cut away from them; their surface was smooth in places, hot, and almost comfortable. Callie lay down and dozed. But as though the walls of the farmhouse had dissolved to let her see through into its rooms, she believed she saw the woman who owned the house—stretched out on a chaste, white-painted bed, her plain head resting on a white pillow, her eyes closed, with the comfortable sounds of insects, birds, and an occasional passing car floating through the window. Soon she would get up and bake banana bread.

Callie opened her eyes, and all around her the squares, rectangles, and trapezoids of the outcropping rock towered or dropped away, like a ruin. Over the tops of the rocks, high and low, sumac was growing, peering out like Indians. It was a wild shrub with long-angling branches, lozenge-shaped leaves, and squat, strong candles of dark brown, with the look of thick wax drippings. After frost, these would turn bright and the leaves would burn red. They were waiting for that to happen, she guessed, as the woman on the bed upstairs in the house was waiting for her napping hour to pass so she could get up and bake. And she, Callie, was waiting, but waiting for Jean-Pierre was not to be compared with other kinds. Everybody and everything, she thought, was waiting, in one way or another. Now she was waiting for Simon Weiss as well, because he had gone somewhere, too.

Callie stood, and wandered farther down through the quarry, which deepened. The path through its center slanted downward, and its chopped-out walls rose higher on either side. A turn to the left and she saw him, standing with his back to her at the edge of a pond. The pond had rocky sides, sloping up out of the water, and she thought the water was from rain, for there was no movement in it, no exit for it. Simon was a waiter, too—she saw that; just by the way he was standing, she saw he was waiting for her.

"Did you go to the police about your husband?" he asked her.

"No, I called up some of his friends, people I had met with him one way or another."

"What did they say?"

"One gave me an address of some relatives up near Trois-Rivières, and another said, 'Oh, Jean-Pierre. But he always come back. *Pas de problème. Vous allez voir!*' "

"My father used to sell religious statues, rosaries, crosses, missals, all that stuff, to all the orders—the French Catholics, that is. Every place with a convent, a shrine, a hospital—Lac Saint-Jean, the Beauce, the Gaspé, Kamouraska—there he was: 'Very good rosaries, blessed by the Pope, hot from Rome.'

Jews get into everything. He said the Québecois, if they get in trouble or get scared, they take to the bush. *Coureurs des bois.* They go to places like Chicoutimi, Rimouski, Rivière du Loup, from there upriver, downriver, into the woods. It was just his idea."

He saw that she was worried—he was troubling her. "You are too gentle for this. All summer it's you I've waited to see. Shiksa. One time at the dinner table, I said out loud, 'The gentle Gentile.' Shana—that's my wife—she heard me. 'A book I'm reading, nothing important,' I said. Now the summer's running out. I can't stop it. I've got no job still. Nor money. My wife works. I live in shame. Yesterday I thought, She likes New England, so take her to New England. What else?"

"The sumac," Callie said. "It's looking at us. Branches, candles, leaves."

He looked around, as if noticing for the first time. "It must remind you of Jean-Pierre. You think he's followed us?"

"Why do you say that?"

"Everything you see. Everything reminds you of Jean-Pierre."

She kicked off her sandals.

"Have you ever read Toynbee?" he asked.

"No, why?" She tested the water with her foot.

"Something he said about societies finding identity, about processes of testing, this way and that way, what to do? The French here might be doing that. Scared, but they have to try. You think so?"

"I don't know." She waded in. The water, being whitish with a chalky suspension, hid the rocks it lay over. The rocks were uneven, some slippery, and toward the pond's center they suddenly dropped away. She drew her foot back, feeling it actually elongate in the pull of an iciness that meant depth at the least, maybe something bottomless. Simon tried to follow her out, but he cut his foot on a rock and sat on the edge with his trouser legs rolled up, washing off threads of blood until they stopped appearing. She waded back, sat near him, and shivered.

"I am disappointed in life," said Simon. "So far, at least, I am disappointed in it. How about you?"

"Hush! Look!" said Callie.

Standing at a good distance, just at the bend of the path between the rocks, was a tall woman in a plain, straight-cut dress, with dark hair. On the instant of their looking, she turned and walked away, vanishing.

"I think that's her," said Simon.

"The one your mother stayed with?"

"I think so, but I can't remember her name."

"I think it's Emily Dickinson," said Callie.

They gathered their things together: time to go. The last savage glare of the sun shot at them from the high cut of the quarry's cliff, where a single frond of sumac, like an outspread hand, sprang up at it. Then the light calmed. The sky was clear, the blueness of the air continuing downward, blue almost to the milky surface of the pool. Callie walked with him, remembering the water, its thickness and sudden cold. The quarry grew larger around them, and they a small pair passing from it. When they passed the farmhouse, a voice called out from inside. "Listen, don't take your brother down there anymore."

"I won't," Callie called back.

"I asked you before, do you remember?"

"I just forgot," she called.

"He was the one that brought those girls and all that beer."

"I'm sorry, I forgot," she answered, but to him she said, "If she's your mother's friend, don't you want to go and talk to her?"

"I wonder if this is the place," he said, walking on. "I don't remember any quarry."

"You'd have to remember that," she said, thinking of its

awesome finalities—the silent, stony walls, the path that ended at the dead pool's edge, the watchful sumac high and low. "That was 'the atom's tomb,' " she said.

"So now we know."

Back in Montreal, she made him let her out a block from where she lived.

"You didn't know it, maybe, Callie," said Simon, gnawing a fingernail that was already fractional, "but down there in the quarry I wanted to love you. It was very much on my mind. When that woman appeared, the feelings got away."

"It's O.K.," she said, and took his hand from his mouth and held it.

"That damned Emily," he said. "Let's go back again."

"They're expecting you, aren't they? Your family and all."

"I know it's late. Time to go."

She got out, promising to call him. It was almost dark.

When she rounded the corner into her own street and looked up, she saw the apartment windows, and a light inside, toward the back. Frightened, she stopped for a moment, considering. Some other waiting was going on up there.

Just over the threshold—lobby, elevator, and corridor all passed—her forward motion failed her. She stood where she was, the door still ajar at her back, as if on the edge of a forest she did not dare to enter. The arched spring of the cat out of a closet was so startling she cried out. Its back seemed to stand for a moment in the air, the cool silver the color of fear. It landed right in the middle of the living-room rug. It must have been crouched on a high shelf, hidden in the dark. It let out a small noise and trotted toward her, raising its face in a voiceless cry. Coming into the room, she bent to pick it up, but its heart was beating all over it, much like her own. It raced to her shoulder, clinging, its claws coming sharp into her skin, and sharper still when a step sounded from the kitchen and Jean-Pierre walked in. He saw them both, the cat and her, and stopped dead still.

At a wary, Indian distance, the two of them stood in silent confrontation.

"Where were you?" he finally asked, speaking English.

"I work in a library. I have all summer. Where were you?"

"Une grosse question." He turned aside, made to do so, she thought, by the cat, who had reared up on stiff paws above her head and spat at him. He had not changed at all, Callie thought, extravagantly relieved, for her dreams had brought him to her hurt and broken. He looked tired and was wearing a suit she'd never seen, that was all.

"Where did you get that cat?"

"I didn't get him. He just came here after you left. He wanted to stay with me. I don't know why."

"He stays because he belongs to you," said Jean-Pierre. *"Il est à toi. Il le sait bien."*

She did not answer.

"If he left, he would come back," he pursued in French. Then, in English, "He knows his place. *Et sa maîtresse.* He knows."

"*Et toi?* What is it you know?"

He spread his hands. "All that I know, *mon ange,* I'd like to tell you. *C'est une histoire assez longue.*"

"You went back to your people. Down the river. Around Quebec."

He was looking at her with anxious desire, at the long hair the cat guarded. Her own desire was a gravid body sleeping. She went past him into the bedroom. Once alone with her, the cat jumped down but stayed close. She washed her face and hands, changed her blouse, and brushed her hair. Rimouski, Chicoutimi, she thought, steadying her breath against the strange names. Kamouraska, Rivière du Loup . . . They fell through her thoughts as thick as snow. Tadoussac . . . Lac Saint-Jean . . . Saint-Gabriel . . . Why did you go? What did you learn? He had promised to tell her. When he told her, would she know?

The moment when I turned back, she wanted to say to him, was in a deserted quarry, beside a stone-dead pool, with another man's voice talking, sumac looking down; where, when you turned, were you? She imagined his secret face, most private in that instant, and knew she would seek out the moment under his words, hidden in the thicket of whatever he would talk about.

The cat still hung about her ankles. "I won't leave you," she knelt to say. "It's only Jean-Pierre. He lives here too."

THE COUSINS

I could say that on the train from Milan to Florence I recalled the events of thirty summers ago and the curious affair of my cousin Eric. But it wouldn't be true. I had Eric somewhere in my mind all the time, a constant. But he was never quite definable, and like a puzzle no one could ever solve, he bothered me. More recently, I had felt a restlessness I kept trying without success to lose, and I had begun to see Eric as its source.

The incident that had triggered my journey to find him had occurred while lunching with my cousin Ben in New York, his saying, "I always thought in some way I can't pin down—it was your fault we lost Eric." Surprising myself, I had felt stricken at the remark as though the point of a cold dagger had reached a vital spot. There was a story my cousins used to tell, out in the swing, under the shade trees, about a man found dead with no clues but a bloody shirt and a small pool of water on the floor beside him. Insoluble mystery. Answer. He was stabbed with a Dagger of Ice! I looked up from eating bay scallops. "*My* fault! Why?"

Ben gave some vague response, something about Eric's

need for staying indifferent, no matter what. "But he could do that in spite of me," I protested. "Couldn't he?"

"Oh, forget it." He filled my glass. "I sometimes speculate out loud, Ella Mason."

Just before that he had remarked how good I was looking—good for a widow just turned fifty, I think he meant. But once he got my restlessness so stirred up, I couldn't lose it. I wanted calming, absolving. I wanted freeing and only Eric—since it was he I was in some way to blame for, or he to blame for me—could do that. So I came alone to Italy, where I had not been for thirty years.

For a while in Milan, spending a day or so to get over jet lag, I wondered if the country existed anymore in the way I remembered it. Maybe, even back then, I had invented the feelings I had, the magic I had wanted to see. But on the train to Florence, riding through the June morning, I saw a little town from the window, in the bright, slightly hazy distance. I don't know what town it was. It seemed built all of a whitish stone, with a church, part of a wall cupping around one side and a piazza with a few people moving across it. With that sight and its stillness in the distance and its sudden vanishing as the train whisked past, I caught my breath and knew it had all been real. So it still was, and would remain. I hadn't invented anything.

From the point of that glimpsed white village, spreading outward through my memory, all its veins and arteries, the whole summer woke up again, like a person coming out of a trance.

Sealed, fleet, the train was rocking on. I closed my eyes with the image of the village, lying fresh and gentle against my mind's eye. I didn't have to try, to know that everything from then would start living now.

Once at the hotel and unpacked, with my dim lamp and clean bathroom and view of a garden—Eric had reserved all this for me: we had written and talked—I placed my telephone call. *"Pronto,"* said the strange voice. "Signor Mason," I said. "Ella Mason, is that you?" So there was his own Alabama voice, not a bit changed. "It's me," I said, "tired from the train." "Take a nap. I'll call for you at seven."

Whatever Southerners are, there are ways they don't change, the same manners to count on, the same tone of voice, never lost. Eric was older than I by about five years. I remember he taught me to play tennis, not so much how to play, because we all knew that, as what not to do. Tennis manners. I had wanted to keep running after balls for him when they rolled outside the court, but he stopped me from doing that. He would take them up himself, and stroke them underhand to his opponent across the net. "Once in a while's all right," he said. "Just go sit down, Ella Mason." It was his way of saying there was always a right way to do things. I was only about ten. The next year it was something else I was doing wrong, I guess, because I always had a lot to learn. My cousins had this constant fondness about them. They didn't mind telling what they knew.

Waking in Florence in the late afternoon, wondering where I was, then catching on. The air was still and warm. It had the slight haziness in the brightness that I had seen from the train, and which I had lost in the bother of the station, the hastening of the taxi through the annoyance of crowds and narrow streets, across the Arno. The little hotel, a *pensione,* really, was out near the Pitti Palace.

Even out so short a distance from the center, Florence could seem the town of thirty years ago, or even the way it must have been in the Brownings' time, narrow streets and the light that way and the same flowers and gravel walks in the gardens. Not that much changes if you build with stone. Not until I saw the stooped gray man hastening through the *pensione* door did I get slapped by change, in the face. How could Eric look like that? Not that I hadn't had photographs, letters. He at once circled me, embracing, my head right against him, sight of him temporarily lost in that. As was his of me, I realized, thinking of all those lines I must have added, along with twenty extra pounds and a high count of gray in the reddish-brown hair. So we both got bruised by the sight of each other, and hung together to blot each other out and soothe the hurt.

The shock was only momentary. We were too glad to see each other. We went some streets away, parked his car, and climbed about six flights of stone stairs. His place had a view over the river, first a great luxurious room opening past the entrance, then a terrace beyond. There were paintings, dark furniture, divans and chairs covered with good, rich fabric. A blond woman's picture in a silver frame—poised, lovely. Through an alcove, the glimpse of an impressive desk, spread with papers, a telephone. You'd be forced to say he'd done well.

"It's cooler outside on the terrace," Eric said, coming in with drinks. "You'll like it over the river." So we went out there and talked. I was getting used to him now. His profile hadn't changed. It was firm, regular, Cousin Lucy Skinner's all over. That was his mother. We were just third cousins. Kissing kin. I sat answering questions. How long would it take, I wondered, to get around to the heart of things? To whatever had carried him away, and what had brought me here?

We'd been brought up together back in Martinsville, Alabama, not far from Birmingham. There was our connection and not much else in that little town of seven thousand and something. Or so we thought. And so we would have everybody else think. We did, though, despite a certain snobbishness—or maybe because of it—have a lot of fun. There were three leading families, in some way "connected." Eric and I had had the same great-grandfather. His mother's side were distant cousins, too. Families who had gone on living around there, through the centuries. Many were the stories and wide-ranged the knowledge, though it was mainly of local interest. As a way of living, I always told myself, it might have gone on for us, too, right through the present and into an endless future, except for that trip we took that summer.

It started with ringing phones.

Eric calling one spring morning to say, "You know the idea Jamie had last night down at Ben's about going to Europe? Well, why don't we do it?"

"This summer's impossible," I said, "I'm supposed to help Papa in the law office."

"He can get Sister to help him—" That was Eric's sister Chessie, one way of making sure she didn't decide to go with us. "You all will have to pay her a little, but she wants a job. Think it over, Ella Mason, but not for very long. Mayfred wants to, and Ben sounds serious, and there's Jamie and you makes five. Ben knows a travel agent in Birmingham. He thinks we might even get reduced rates, but we have to hurry. We should have thought this up sooner."

His light voice went racing on. He read a lot. I didn't even have to ask him where we'd go. He and Ben would plan it, both young men who had studied things, knew things, read, talked, quoted. We'd go where they wanted to go, love what they planned, admire them. Jamie was younger, my uncle Gale's son, but he was forming that year—he was becoming grown-up. Would he be like them? There was nothing else to be but like them, if at all possible. No one in his right mind would question that.

Ringing phones . . . "Oh, I'm thrilled to death! What did your folks say? It's not all that expensive what with the exchange, not as much as staying here and going somewhere like the Smokies. You can pay for the trip over with what you'd save."

We meant to go by ship. Mayfred, who read up on the

latest things, wanted to fly, but nobody would hear to it. The boat was what people talked about when they mentioned their trip. It was a phrase: "On the boat going over . . . On the boat coming back . . ." The train was what we'd take to New York, or maybe we could fly. Mayfred, once redirected, began to plan everybody's clothes. She knew what things were drip-dry and crush-proof. On and on she forged through slick-paged magazines.

"It'll take the first two years of law practice to pay for it, but it might be worth it," said Eric. *"J'ai très hâte d'y aller,"* said Ben. The little French he knew was a lot more than ours.

Eric was about twenty-five that summer, just finishing law school, having been delayed a year or so by his army service. I wasn't but nineteen. The real reason I had hesitated about going was a boy from Tuscaloosa I'd been dating up at the university last fall, but things were running down with him, even though I didn't want to admit it. I didn't love him so much as I wanted him to love me, and that's no good, as Eric himself told me. Ben was riding high, having gotten part of his thesis accepted for publication in the *Sewanee Review*. He had written on "The Lost Ladies of Edgar Allan Poe" and this piece was the chapter on "Ulalume." I pointed out they weren't so much lost as dead, or sealed up half-dead in tombs, but Ben didn't see the humor in that.

The syringa was blooming that year, and the spirea and bridal wreath. The flags had come and gone but not the wisteria, prettier than anybody could remember. All our mothers doted on their yards, while not a one of us ever raised so much as a petunia. No need to. We called each other from bower to bower. Our cars kept floating us through soft spring twilights. Travel folders were everywhere and Ben had scratched up enough French grammars to go around so we could practice some phrases. He thought we ought at least to know how to order in a restaurant and ask for stationery and soap in a hotel. Or buy stamps and find the bathroom.

He was on to what to say to cabdrivers when somebody mentioned that we were spending all this time on French without knowing a word of Italian. What did *they* say for Hello, or How much does it cost? or Which way to the post office? Ben said we didn't have time for Italian. He thought the people you had to measure up to were the French. What Italians thought of you didn't matter all that much. We were generally over at Eric's house because his mother was away visiting his married sister Edith and the grandchildren, and Eric's father couldn't have cared less if we had drinks of real whiskey in the evening. In fact, he was often out playing poker and doing the same thing himself.

The Masons had a grand house. (Mason was Mama's maiden name and so my middle one.) I loved the house especially when nobody was in it but all of us. It was white, two-story with big high-ceilinged rooms. The tree branches laced across it by moonlight, so that you could only see patches of it. Mama was always saying they ought to thin things out, take out half the shrubs and at least three trees (she would even say which trees), but Cousin Fred, Eric's father, liked all that shaggy growth. Once inside, the house took you over—it liked us all—and we were often back in the big kitchen after supper fixing drinks or sitting out on the side porch making jokes and talking about Europe. One evening it would be peculiar things about the English, and the next, French food, how much we meant to spend on it, and so on. We had a long argument about Mont St.-Michel, which Ben had read about in a book by Henry Adams; but everybody else, though coaxed into reading at least part of the book, thought it was too far up there and we'd better stick around Paris. We hoped Ben would forget it: he was bossy when he got his head set. We just wanted to see Ver-sigh and Fontaine-blow.

"We could stop off in the southern part of France on our way to Italy" was Eric's idea. "It's where all the painting comes from."

"I'd rather see the paintings," said Mayfred. "They're mostly in Paris, aren't they?"

"That's not the point," said Ben.

Jamie was holding out for one night in Monte Carlo.

Jamie had shot up like a weed a few years back and had just never filled out. He used to regard us all as slightly opposed to him, as though none of us could possibly want to do what he most liked. He made, at times, common cause with Mayfred, who was kin to us only by a thread, so complicated I wouldn't dream of untangling it.

Mayfred was a grand-looking girl. Ben said it once: "She's got class." He said that when we were first debating whether to ask her along or not (if not her, then my roommate from Texas would be invited), and had decided that we had to ask Mayfred or smother her because we couldn't have stopped talking about our plans if our lives depended on it and she was always around. The afternoon Ben made that remark about her, we were just the three of us—Ben, Eric, and me—out to help Mama about the annual lining of the tennis court, and had stopped to sit on a bench, being sweaty and needing some shade to catch our breath in. So he said that in his meditative way, hitting the edge of a tennis racket on the ground between his feet and occasionally sighting down it to see if it had warped during a winter in the press. And Eric, after a silence in which he looked off to one side until you thought he hadn't heard (this being his way), said: "You'd think the rest of us had no class at all." "Of course we have, we just never mention it," said Ben. So we'd clicked again. I always loved that to happen.

Mayfred had a boyfriend named Donald Bailey, who came over from Georgia and took her out every Saturday night. He was fairly nice-looking was about all we knew, and Eric thought he was dumb.

"I wonder how Mayfred is going to get along without Donald," Ben said.

"I can't tell if she really likes him or not," I said. "She never talks about him."

"She just likes to have somebody," Ben said tersely, a thread of disapproval in his voice, the way he could do.

Papa was crazy about Mayfred. "You can't tell what she thinks about anything and she never misses a trick," he said. His unspoken thought was that I was always misjudging things. "Don't you *see,* Ella Mason," he would say. But are things all that easy to see?

"Do you remember," I said to Eric on the terrace, this long after, "much about Papa?"

"What about him?"

"He wanted me to be different, some way."

"Different how?"

"More like Mayfred," I said, and laughed, making it clear that I was deliberately shooting past the mark, because really I didn't know where it was.

"Well," said Eric, looking past me out to where the lights were brightening along the Arno, the towers standing out clearly in the dusky air, "I liked you the way you were."

It was good, hearing him say that. The understanding that I wanted might not come. But I had a chance, I thought, and groped for what to say, when Eric rose to suggest dinner, a really good restaurant he knew, not far away; we could even walk.

". . . Have you been to the Piazza? No, of course, you haven't had time. Well, don't go. It's covered with tourists and pigeon shit; they've moved all the real statues inside except the Cellini. Go look at that and leave quick. . . ."

"You must remember Jamie, though, how he put his head in his hands our first day in Italy and cried, 'I was just being nice to him and he took all the money!' Poor Jamie, I think something else was wrong with him, not just a couple of thousand lire."

"You think so, but what?"

"Well, Mayfred had made it plain that Donald was her choice of a man, though not present. And of course there was Ben . . ." My voice stopped just before I stepped on a crack in the sidewalk.

". . . Ben had just got into Yale that spring before we left. He was hitching to a *fu*ture, man!" It was just as well Eric said it.

"So that left poor Jamie out of everything, didn't it? He was young, another year in college to go, and nothing really outstanding about him, so he thought, and nobody he could pair with."

"There were you and me."

"You and me," I repeated. It would take a book to describe how I said that. Half-question, half-echo, a total wondering what to say next. How, after all, did *he* mean it? It wasn't like me to say nothing. "He might just have wondered what *we* had?"

"He might have," said Eric. In the corner of the white-plastered restaurant, where he was known and welcomed, he was enjoying grilled chicken and artichokes. But suddenly he put down his fork, a pause like a solstice. He looked past my shoulder: Eric's way.

"Ben said it was my fault we 'lost' you. That's how he put it. He told me that in New York, the last time I saw him, six weeks ago. He wouldn't explain. Do you understand what he meant?"

" 'Lost,' am I? It's news to me."

"Well, you know, not at home. Not even in the States. Is that to do with me?"

"We'll go back and talk." He pointed to my plate. "Eat your supper, Ella Mason," he said.

My mind began wandering pleasantly. I fell to remembering the surprise Mayfred had handed us all when we got to New York. We had come up on the train, having gone up to Chattanooga to catch the Southern. Three days in New York and we would board the *Queen Mary* for Southampton. "Too romantic for anything," Mama had warbled on the phone. ("Elsa Stephens says, 'Too romantic for anything,' " she said at the table. "No, Mama, you said that, I heard you." "Well, I don't care who said it, it's true.") On the second afternoon in New York, Mayfred vanished with something vague she had to do. "Well, you know she's always tracking down dresses," Jamie told me. "I think she wants her hair restyled somewhere," I said. But not till we were having drinks in the hotel bar before dinner did Mayfred show up with Donald Bailey! She had, in addition to Donald, a new dress and a new hair-style, and the three things looked to me about of equal value, I was thinking, when she suddenly announced with an ear-splitting smile: "We're married!" There was a total silence, broken at last by Donald, who said with a shuffling around of feet and gestures, "It's just so I could come along with y'all, if y'all don't mind." "Well," said Ben, at long last, "I guess you both better sit down." Another silence followed, broken by Eric, who said he guessed it was one excuse for having champagne.

Mayfred and Donald had actually gotten married across the state line in Georgia two weeks before. Mayfred didn't want to discuss it because, she said, everybody was so taken up with talking about Europe, she wouldn't have been able to get a word in edgewise. "You better go straight and call yo' Mama," said Ben. "Either you do, or I will."

Mayfred's smile fell to ashes and she sloshed out champagne. "She can't do a thing about it till we get back home! She'll want me to explain everything. Don't y'all make me . . . please!"

I noticed that so far Mayfred never made common cause with any one of us, but always spoke to the group: Y'all. It also occurred to me both then and now that that was what had actually saved her. If one of us had gotten involved in pleading for her with Ben, he would have overruled us. But Mayfred, a lesser cousin, was keeping a distance. She could have said—and I thought she was on the verge of it—that she'd gone to a lot of trouble to satisfy us; she might have just brought him along without benefit of ceremony.

So we added Donald Bailey. Unbeknownst to us, reservations had been found for him, and though he had to share a four-berth, tourist-class cabin with three strange men, after a day out certain swaps were effected, and he wound up in second class with Mayfred. Eric overheard a conversation between Jamie and Donald which he passed on to me. Jamie: Don't you really think this is a funny way to spend a honeymoon? Donald: It was just the best I could do.

He was a polite squarish sort of boy with heavy, dark lashes. He and Mayfred used to stroll off together regularly after the noon meal on board. It was a serene crossing, for the weather cleared two days out of New York and we could spend a lot of time on deck playing shuffleboard and betting on races with wooden horses run by the purser. (I forgot to say everybody in our family but Ben's branch were inveterate gamblers and had played poker in the club car all the way up to New York on the train.) After lunch every day Mayfred got seasick and Donald in true husbandly fashion would take her to whichever side the wind was not blowing against and let her throw up neatly over the rail, like a cat. Then she'd be all right. Later, when you'd see them together they were always talking and laughing. But with us she was quiet and trim, with her fashion-blank look, and he was just quiet. He all but said "Ma'am" and "Sir." As a result of Mayfred's marriage, I was thrown a lot with Eric, Ben, and Jamie. "I think one of you ought to get married," I told them. "Just temporarily, so I wouldn't feel like the only girl." Ben promised to take a look around and Eric seemed not to have heard. It was Jamie who couldn't joke about it. He had set himself to make a pair, in some sort of way, with Mayfred, I felt. I don't know how seriously he took her. Things run deep in our family—that's what you have to know. Eric said out of the blue, "I'm wondering when they had time to see each other; Mayfred spent all her time with us." (We were prowling through the Tate Gallery.) "Those Saturday-night dates," I said, studying Turner. At times she would show up with us, without Donald, not saying much, attentive and smooth, making company. Ben told her she looked Parisian.

Eric and Ben were both well into manhood that year, and were so future conscious they seemed to be talking about it even when they weren't saying anything. Ben had decided on literature, had finished a master's at Sewanee and was going on to Yale, while Eric had just stood law school exams at Emory. He was in some considerable debate about whether he shouldn't go into literary studies, too, for unlike Ben, whose interest was scholarly, he wanted to be a writer, and he had some elaborate theory that actually studying literature reduced the possibility of your being able to write it. Ben saw his point, and though he did not entirely agree, felt that law might just be the right choice—it put you in touch with how things actually worked. "Depending, of course, on whether you tend to fiction or poetry. It would be more important in regard to fiction because the facts matter so much more." So they trod along ahead of us—through London sights, their heels coming down in tandem. They might have been two dons in an Oxford street, debating something. Next to come were Jamie and me, and behind, at times, Donald and Mayfred.

I was so fond of Jamie those days. I felt for him in a family way, almost motherly. When he said he wanted a night in Monte Carlo, I sided with him, just as I had about going at least once to the picture show in London. Why shouldn't he have his way? Jamie said one museum a day was enough. I felt the same. He was all different directions with himself: too tall, too thin, big feet, small head. Once I caught his hand: "Don't worry," I said, "everything good will happen to you."

The way I remember it, we looked back just then, and there came Mayfred, alone. She caught up with us. We were standing on a street corner near Hyde Park and, for a change, it was sunny. "Donald's gone home," she said, cheerfully. "He said tell you all goodbye."

We hadn't seen her all day. We were due to leave for France the next morning. She told us, for one thing, that Donald had persistent headaches and thought he ought to see about it. He seemed, as far as we could tell, to have limitless supplies of money, and had once taken us all for dinner at the Savoy, where only Mayfred could move into all that glitter with an air of belonging to it. He didn't like to bring up his illness and trouble us, Mayfred explained. "Maybe it was too much honeymoon for him," Eric speculated to me in private. I had to say I didn't know. I did know that Jamie had come out like the English sun—unexpected, but marvelously bright.

I held out for Jamie and Monte Carlo. He wasn't an intellectual like Ben and Eric. He would listen while they finished up a bottle of wine and then would start looking around the restaurant. "That lady didn't have anything but snails and bread," he would say, or, of a couple leaving, "He didn't even know that girl when they came in." He was just being a small-town boy. But with Mayfred he must have been different, she laughed so much. "What do they talk about?" Ben asked me, perplexed. "Ask them," I advised. "You think they'd tell me?" "I doubt it," I said. "They wouldn't know what to say," I added; "they would just tell you the last things they said." "You mean like, Why do they call it the Seine if they don't seine for fish in it? Real funny."

Jamie got worried about Mayfred in Paris because the son of the hotel owner, a young Frenchman so charming he looked like somebody had made him up whole cloth, wanted to take her out. She finally consented, with some trepidation on our part, especially from Ben, who in this case posed as her uncle, with strict orders from her father. The Frenchman, named Paul something, was not disturbed in the least: Ben fit right in with his ideas of how things ought to be. So Mayfred went out with him, looking, except for her sunny hair, more French than the natives—we all had to admit being proud of her. I also had invitations, but none so elegant. "What happened?" we all asked, the next day. "Nothing," she insisted. "We just went to this little nightclub place near some school . . . begins with an 'S.' " "The Sorbonne," said Ben, whose bemusement, at that moment, peaked. "Then what?" Eric asked. "Well, nothing. You just eat something, then talk and have some wine and get up and dance. They dance different. Like this." She locked her hands together in the air. "He thought he couldn't talk good enough for me in English, but it was O.K." Paul sent her some *marrons glacés,* which she opened on the train south, and Jamie munched one with happy jaws. Paul had not suited him. It was soon after that, he and Mayfred began their pairing off. In Jamie's mind we were moving on to Monte Carlo, and had been ever since London. The first thing he did was find out how to get to the Casino.

He got dressed for dinner better than he had since the Savoy. Mayfred seemed to know a lot about the gambling places, but her attitude was different from his. Jamie was bird-dogging toward the moment; she was just curious. "I've got to trail along," Eric said after dinner, "just to see the show." "Not only that," said Ben, "we might have to stop him in case he gets too carried away. We might have to bail him out." When we three, following up the rear (this was Jamie's night), entered the discreetly glittering rotunda, stepped on thick carpets beneth the giant, multiprismed chandeliers, heard the low chant of the croupier, the click of roulette, the rustle of money at the bank, and saw the bright, rhythmic movements of dealers and wheels and stacks of chips, it was still Jamie's face that was the sight worth watching. All was mirrored there. Straight from the bank, he visited card tables and wheels, played the blind dealing-machine—chemin de fer—and finally turned, a small sum to the good, to his real goal: roulette. Eric had by then lost a hundred francs or so, but I had about made up for it, and Ben wouldn't play at all. "It's my Presbyterian side," he told us. His mother had been one of those. "It's known as 'riotous living,' " he added.

It wasn't riotous at first, but it was before we left, because Jamie, once he advanced on the roulette, with Mayfred beside him—she was wearing some sort of gold blouse with long peasant sleeves and a low-cut neck she had picked up cheap in a shop that afternoon, and was not speaking to him but instead, with a gesture so European you'd think she'd been born there, slipping her arm through his just at the wrist and leaning her head back a little—was giving off the glow of somebody so magically aided by a presence every inch his own that he could not and would not lose. Jamie, in fact, looked suddenly aristocratic, overbred, like a Russian greyhound or a Rumanian prince. Both Eric and I suspended our own operations to watch. The little ball went clicking round as the wheel spun. Black. Red. And red. Back to black. All wins. People stopped to look on. Two losses, then the wins again, continuing. Mayfred had a look of curious bliss around her mouth—she looked like a cat in process of a good purr. The take mounted.

Ben called Eric and me aside. "It's going on all night," he said. We all sat down at the little gold-and-white-marble bar and ordered Perriers.

"Well," said Eric, "what did he start with?"

"Couldn't have been much," said Ben, "if I didn't miss anything. He didn't change more than a couple of hundred at the desk."

"That sounds like a lot to me," said Eric.

"I mean," said Ben, "it won't ruin him to lose it all."

"You got us into this," said Eric to me.

"Oh, gosh, I know it. But look. He's having the time of his life."

Everybody in the room had stopped to watch Jamie's luck. Some people were laughing. He had a way of stopping everybody and saying: "What's *that* mean?" as if only English could or ought to be spoken in the entire world. Some man near us said, *"Le cavalier de l'Okla-hum,"* and another answered, *"Du Texas, plutôt."* Then he took three more in a row and they were silent.

It was Mayfred who made him stop. It seemed like she had an adding machine in her head. All of a sudden she told him something, whispered in his ear. When he shook his head, she caught his hands. When he pulled away, she grabbed his arm. When he lifted his arm, she came up with it, right off the floor. For a minute I thought they were both going to fall over into the roulette wheel.

"You got to stop, Jamie!" Mayfred said in the loudest Alabama voice I guess they'd ever be liable to hear that side of the ocean. It was curdling, like cheering for 'Bama against Ole Miss in the Sugar Bowl. "I don't have to stop!" he yelled right back. "If you don't stop," Mayfred shouted, "I'll never speak to you again, Jamie Marshall, as long as I live!"

The croupier looked helpless, and everybody in the room was turning away like they didn't see us, while through a thin door at the end of the room, a man in black tie was approaching who could only be called the "management." Ben was already pulling Jamie toward the bank. "Cash it in now, we'll go along to another one . . . maybe tomorrow we can . . ." It was like pulling a stubborn calf across the lot, but he finally made it with some help from Mayfred, who stood over Jamie while he counted everything to the last sou. She made us all take a taxi back to the hotel because she said it was common knowledge when you won a lot they sent somebody out to rob you, first thing. Next day she couldn't rest till she got Jamie to change the francs into traveler's checks, U.S. He had won well over two thousand dollars, all told.

The next thing, as they saw it, was to keep Jamie out of the Casino. Ben haggled a long time over lunch, and Eric, who was good at scheming, figured out a way to get up to a village in the hills where there was a Matisse chapel he couldn't live longer without seeing. And Mayfred took to hand-holding and even gave Jamie on the sly (I caught her at it) a little nibbling kiss or two. What did they care? I wondered. I thought he should get to go back and lose it all.

It was up in the mountain village that afternoon that I blundered in where I'd rather not have gone. I had come out of the chapel where Ben and Eric were deep in discussion of whether Matisse could ever place in the front rank of French art, and had climbed part of the slope nearby where a narrow stair ran up to a small square with a dry stone fountain. Beyond that, in the French manner, was a small café with a striped awning and a few tables. From somewhere I heard Jamie's voice, saying, "I know, but what'd you do it for?" "Well, what does anybody do anything for? I wanted to." "But what would you want to *for,* Mayfred?" "Same reason you'd want to, sometime." "I wouldn't want to, except to be with you." "Well, I'm right here, aren't I? You got your wish." "What I wish is you hadn't done it." It was bound to be marrying Donald that he meant. He had a frown that would come at times between his light eyebrows. I came to associate it with Mayfred. How she was running him. When they stepped around the corner of the path, holding hands (immediately dropped), I saw that frown. Did I have to dislike Mayfred, the way she was acting? The funny thing was, I didn't even know.

We lingered around the village and ate there and the bus was late, so we never made it back to the casinos. By then all Jamie seemed to like was being with Mayfred, and the frown disappeared.

Walking back to the apartment, passing darkened doorways, picking up pieces of Eric's past like fragments in the street.

". . . And then you did or didn't marry her, and she died and left you the legacy . . ."

"Oh, we did get married, all right, the anticlimax of a number of years. I wish you could have known her. The marriage was civil. She was afraid the family would cause a row if she wanted to leave me anything. That was when she knew she hadn't long to live. Not that it was any great fortune. She had some property out near Pasquallo, a little town near here. I sold it. I had to fight them in court for a while, but it did eventually clear up."

"You've worked, too, for this other family . . . ?"

"The Rinaldi. You must have got all this from Ben, though maybe I wrote you, too. They were friends of hers. It's all connections here, like anywhere else. Right now they're all at the sea below Genoa. I'd be there too, but I'd some business in town, and you were coming. It's the export side I've helped them with. I do know English, and a little law, in spite of all."

"So it's a regular Italian life," I mused, climbing stairs, entering the *salotto,* where I saw again the woman's picture in a silver frame. Was that her, the one who had died? "Was she blond?" I asked, moving as curiously through his life as a child through a new room.

"Giana, you mean? No, part Sardinian, dark as they come. Oh, you mean her. No, that's Lisa, one of the Rinaldi, Paolo's sister . . . that's him up there."

I saw then, over a bookshelf, a man's enlarged photo: tweed jacket, pipe, all in the English style.

"So what else, Ella Mason?" His voice was amused at me.

"She's pretty," I said.

"Very pretty," he agreed.

We drifted out to the terrace once more.

It is time I talked about Ben and Eric, about how it was with me and with them and with the three of us.

When I look back on pictures of myself in those days, I see a girl in shorts, weighing a few pounds more than she thought she should, low-set, with a womanly cast to her body, chopped-off reddish hair, and a wide, freckled, almost boyish grin, happy to be posing between two tall boys, who happened to be her cousins, smiling their white, tentative smiles. Ben and Eric. They were smart. They were fun. They did everything right. And most of all, they admitted me. I was the audience they needed.

I had to run to keep up. I read Poe because of Ben's thesis; and Wallace Stevens because Eric liked his poetry. I even, finding him referred to at times, tried to read Plato. (Ben studied Greek.) But what I did was not of much interest to them. Still, they wanted me around. Sometimes Ben made a point of "conversing" with me—what courses, what books, etc.—but he made me feel like a high-school student. Eric, seldom bothering with me, was more on my level when he did. To one another, they talked at a gallop. Literature turned them on, their ideas flowed, ran back and forth like a current. I loved hearing them.

I think of little things they did. Such as Ben's coming back from Sewanee with a small Roman statue, copy of something Greek—Apollo, I think—just a fragment, a head, turned aside, shoulders and a part of a back. His professor had given it to him as a special mark of favor. He set it on his favorite pigeonhole desk, to stay there, it would seem, for always, to be seen always by the rest of us—by me.

Such as Eric ordering his "secondhand but good condition" set of Henry James's novels with prefaces, saying, "I know this is corny but it's what I wanted," making space in his Mama's old upright secretary with glass-front bookshelves above, and my feeling that they'd always be there. I strummed my fingers across the spines lettered in gold. Someday I would draw down one or another to read them. No hurry.

Such as the three of us packing Mama's picnic basket (it seems my folks were the ones with the practical things—tennis court, croquet set: though Jamie's set up a badminton court at one time, it didn't take) to take to a place called Beulah Woods for a spring day in the sun near a creek where water ran clear over white limestone, then plunged off into a swimming hole. Ben sat on a bedspread reading Ransom's poetry aloud and we gossiped about the latest town scandal, involving a druggist, a real estate deal where some property went cheap to him, though it seemed now that his wife had been part of the bargain, being lent out on a regular basis to the man who sold him the property. The druggist was a newcomer. A man we all knew in town had been after the property and was now threatening to sue. "Do you think it was written in the deed, so many nights a week she goes off to work the property out?" Ben speculated. "Do you think they calculated the interest?" It wasn't the first time our talk had run toward sexual things; in a small town, secrets didn't often get kept for long.

More than once I'd dreamed that someday Ben or Eric would ask me somewhere alone. A few years before the picnic, romping through our big old rambling house at twilight with Jamie, who loved playing hide-and-seek, I had run into the guest room, where Ben was standing in the half-dark by the bed. He was looking at something he'd found there in the twilight, some book or ornament, and I mistook him for Jamie and threw my arms around him crying, "Caught you!" We fell over the bed together and rolled for a moment before I knew then it was Ben, but knew I'd wanted it to be; or didn't I really know all along it was Ben, but pretended I didn't? Without a doubt when his weight came down over me, I knew I wanted it to be there. I felt his body, for a moment so entirely present, draw back and up. Then he stood, turning away, leaving. "You better grow up" was what I think he said. Lingering feelings made me want to seek him out the next day or so. Sulky, I wanted to say, "I *am* growing up." But another time he said, "We're cousins, you know."

Eric for a while dated a girl from one of the next towns. She used to ask him over to parties and they would drive to Birmingham sometimes, but he never had her over to Martinsville. Ben, that summer we went to Europe, let it be known he was writing and getting letters from a girl at Sewanee. She was a pianist named Sylvia. "You want to hear music played softly in the 'drawing room,' " I clowned at him. " 'Just a song at twilight.' " "Now, Ella Mason, you behave," he said.

I had boys to take me places. I could flirt and I got a rush at dances and I could go off the next-to-the-highest diving board and was good in doubles. Once I went on strike from Ben and Eric for over a week. I was going with the boy from Tuscaloosa and I had begun to think he was the right one and get ideas. Why fool around with my cousins? But I missed them. I went around one afternoon. They were talking out on the porch. The record player was going inside, something of Berlioz that Ben was on to. They waited till it finished before they'd speak to me. Then Eric, smiling from the depths of a chair, said, "Hey, Ella Mason"; and Ben, getting up to unlatch the screen, said, "Ella Mason, where on earth have you been?" I'd have to think they were glad.

Ben was dark. He had straight, dark-brown hair, dry-looking in the sun, growing thick at the brow, but flat at night when he put a damp comb through it, and darker. It fit close to his head like a monk's hood. He wore large glasses with Lucite rims. Eric had sandy hair, softly appealing and always mussed. He didn't bother much with his looks. In the day they scuffed around in open-throated shirts and loafers, crinkled seersucker pants, or shorts; tennis shoes when they played were always dirty white. At night, when they cleaned up, it was still casual but fresh laundered. But when they dressed, in shirts and ties with an inch of white cuff laid crisp against their brown hands: they were splendid!

"Ella Mason," Eric said, "if that boy doesn't like you, he's not worth worrying about." He had put his arm around me coming out of the picture show. I ought to drop it, a tired romance, but couldn't quite. Not till that moment. Then I did.

"Those boys," said Mr. Felix Gresham from across the street. "Getting time they started earning something 'stead of all time settin' around." He used to come over and tell Mama everything he thought though no kin to anybody. "I reckon there's time enough for that," Mama said. "Now going off to France," said Mr. Gresham, as though that spoke for itself. "Not just France," Mama said, "England, too, and Italy." "Ain't nothing in France," said Mr. Gresham. "I don't know if there is or not," said Mama, "I never have been." She meant that to hush him up, but the truth is, Mr. Gresham might have been to France in World War I. I never thought to ask. Now he's dead.

Eric and Ben. I guess I was in love with both of them. Wouldn't it be nice, I used to think, if one were my brother and the other my brother's best friend, and then I could just quietly and without so much as thinking about it find myself marrying the friend (now which would I choose for which?) and so we could go on forever? At other times, frustrated, I suppose, by their never changing toward me, I would plan on doing something spectacular, finding a Yankee, for instance, so impressive and brilliant and established in some important career, that they'd have to listen to him, learn what he was doing and what he thought and what he knew, while I sat silent and poised throughout the conversation, the cat that ate the cream, though of course too polite to show satisfaction. Fantasies, one by one, would sing to me for a little while.

At Christmas vacation before our summer abroad, just before Ben got accepted to Yale and just while Eric was getting bored with law school, there was a quarrel. I didn't know the details, but they went back to school with things still unsettled among us. I got friendly with Jamie then, more than before. He was down at Tuscaloosa, like me. It's when I got to know Mayfred better, on weekends at home. Why bother with Eric and Ben? It had been a poor season. One letter came from Ben and I answered it, saying that I had come to like Jamie and Mayfred so much; their parents were always giving parties and we were having a grand time. In answer I got a long, serious letter about time passing and what it did, how we must remember that what we had was always going to be part of ourselves. That he thought of jonquils coming up now and how they always looked like jonquils, just absent for a time, and how the roots stayed the same. He was looking forward, he said, to spring and coming home.

Just for fun I sat down and wrote him a love letter. I said he was a fool and a dunce and didn't he know while he was writing out all these ideas that I was a live young woman and only a second cousin and that through the years while he was talking about Yeats, Proust, and Edgar Allan Poe that I was longing to have my arms around him the way they were when we fell over in the bed that twilight romping around with Jamie and why in the ever-loving world couldn't he see me as I was, a live girl, instead of a cousin-spinster, listening to him and Eric make brilliant conversation? Was he trying to turn me into an old maid? Wasn't he supposed, at least, to be intelligent? So why couldn't he see what I was really like? But I didn't mail it. I didn't because, for one thing, I doubted that I meant it. Suppose, by a miracle, Ben said, "You're right, every word." What about Eric? I started dating somebody new at school. I tore the letter up.

Eric called soon after. He just thought it would do him good to say hello. Studying for long hours wasn't his favorite sport. He'd heard from Ben, the hard feelings were over, he was ready for spring holidays already. I said, "I hope to be in town, but I'm really not sure." A week later I forgot a date with the boy I thought I liked. The earlier one showed up again. Hadn't I liked him, after all? How to be sure? I bought a new straw hat, white-and-navy for Easter, with a ribbon down the back, and came home.

Just before Easter, Jamie's parents gave a party for us all. There had been a cold snap and we were all inside, with purplish-red punch, and a buffet laid out. Jamie's folks had this relatively new house, with new carpets and furnishings and the family dismay ran to what a big mortgage they were carrying and how it would never be paid out. Meantime his mother (no kin) looked completely unworried as she arranged tables that seemed to have been copied from magazines. I came alone, having had to help Papa with some typing, and so saw Ben and Eric for the first time, though we'd talked on the phone.

Eric looked older, a little worn. I saw something drawn in the way he laughed, a sort of restraint about him. He was standing aside and looking at a point where no one and nothing were. But he came to when I spoke and gave that laugh and then a hug. Ben was busy "conversing" with a couple in town who had somebody at Sewanee, too. He smoked a pipe now, I noticed, smelly when we hugged. He had soon come to join Eric and me, and it was at that moment, the three of us standing together for the first time since Christmas, and change having been mentioned at least once by way of Ben's letter, that I knew some tension was mounting, bringing obscure moments with it. We turned to one another but did not speak readily about anything. I had thought I was the only one, sensitive to something imagined—having "vapors," as somebody called it—but I could tell we were all at a loss for some reason none of us knew. Because if Ben and Eric knew, articulate as they were, they would have said so. In the silence so suddenly fallen, something was ticking.

Maybe, I thought, they just don't like Martinsville anymore. They always said that parties were dull and squirmed out of them when they could. I lay awake thinking, They'll move on soon; I won't see them again.

It was the next morning Eric called and we all grasped for Europe like the drowning, clinging to what we could.

After Monte Carlo, we left France by train and came down to Florence. The streets were narrow there and we joked about going single-file like Indians. "What I need is moccasins," said Jamie, who was always blundering over the uneven paving stones. At the Uffizi, the second day, Eric, in a trance before Botticelli, fell silent. Could we ever get him to speak again? Hardly a word. Five in number, we leaned over the balustrades along the Arno, all silent then from the weariness of sightseeing, and the heat; and there I heard it once more, the ticking of something hidden among us. Was it to deny it we decided to take the photograph? We had taken a lot, but this one, I think, was special. I have it still. It was in the Piazza Signoria.

"Which monument?" we kept asking. Ben wanted Donatello's lion, and Eric the steps of the Old Palace; Jamie wanted Cosimo I on his horse. I wanted the *Perseus* of Cellini, and Mayfred the *Rape of the Sabines*. So Ben made straws out of toothpicks and we drew and Mayfred won. We got lined up and Ben framed us. Then we had to find somebody, a slim Italian boy as it turned out, to snap us for a few hundred lire. It seemed we were proving something serious and good, and smiled with our straight family smiles, Jamie with his arm around Mayfred, and she with her smart new straw sun hat held to the back of her head, and me between Ben and Eric, arms entwined. A photo outlasts everybody, and this one with the frantic scene behind us, the moving torso of the warrior holding high the prey while we smiled our ordinary smiles—it was a period, the end of a phase.

Not that the photograph itself caused the end of anything. Donald Bailey caused it. He telephoned the *pensione* that night from Atlanta to say he was in the hospital, gravely ill, something they might have to operate for any day, some sort of brain tumor was what they were afraid of. Mayfred said she'd come.

We all got stunned. Ben and Eric and I straggled off together while she and Jamie went to the upstairs sitting room and sat in the corner. "Honest to God," said Eric, "I just didn't know Donald Bailey had a brain." "He had headaches," said Ben. "Oh, I knew he had a head," said Eric, "we could see that."

By night it was settled. Mayfred would fly back from Rome. Once again she got us to promise secrecy—how she did that I don't know, the youngest one and yet not even Ben could prevail on her one way or the other. By now she had spent most of her money. Donald, we knew, was rich; he came of a rich family and had, furthermore, money of his own. So if she wanted to fly back from Rome, the ticket, already purchased, would be waiting for her. Mayfred got to be privileged, in my opinion, because none of us knew her family too well. Her father was a blood cousin but not too highly regarded—he was thought to be a rather silly man who "traveled" and dealt with "all sorts of people"—and her mother was from "off," a Georgia girl, fluttery. If it had been my folks and if I had started all this wild marrying and flying off, Ben would have been on the phone to Martinsville by sundown.

One thing in the Mayfred departure that went without

question: Jamie would go to Rome to see her off. We couldn't have sealed him in or held him with ropes. He had got on to something new in Italy, or so I felt, because where before then had we seen in gallery after gallery, strong men, young and old, with enraptured eyes, enthralled before a woman's painted image, wanting nothing? What he had gotten was an idea of devotion. It fit him. It suited. He would do anything for Mayfred and want nothing. If she had got pregnant and told him she was a virgin, he would have sworn to it before the Inquisition. It could positively alarm you for him to see him satisfied with the feelings he had found. Long after I went to bed, he was at the door or in the corridor with Mayfred, discussing baggage and calling a hotel in Rome to get a reservation for when he saw her off.

Mayfred had bought a lot of things. She had an eye for what she could wear with what, and she would pick up pieces of this and that for putting costumes and accessories together. She had to get some extra luggage and it was Jamie, of course, who promised to see it sent safely to her, through a shipping company in Rome. His two thousand dollars was coming in handy, was all I could think.

Hot, I couldn't sleep, so I went out in the sitting room to find a magazine. Ben was up. The three men usually took a large room together, taking turns for the extra cot. Ever since we got the news, Ben had had what Eric called his "family mood." Now he called me over. "I can't let those kids go down there alone," he said. "They seem like children to me—and Jamie . . . about all he can say is *grazie* and *quanto.*" "Then let's all go," I said, "I've given up sleeping for tonight anyway." "Eric's hooked on Florence," said Ben. "Can't you tell? He counts the cypresses on every knoll. He can spot a Della Robbia a block off. If I make him leave three days early, he'll never forgive me. Besides, our reservations in that hotel can't be changed. We called for Jamie and they're full; he's staying third class somewhere till we all come. I don't mind doing that. Then we'll all meet up just the way we planned, have our week in Rome, and go catch the boat from Naples." "I think they could make it on their own," I said, "it's just that you'd worry every minute." He grinned; "our father for the duration" was what Eric called him. "I know I'm that way," he said.

Another thing was that Ben had been getting little caches of letters at various points along our trek from his girlfriend Sylvia, the one he'd been dating up at Sewanee. She was getting a job in New York that fall which would be convenient to Yale. She wrote a spidery hand on thick rippled stationery, cream-colored, and had promised in her last dispatch, received in Paris, to write to Rome. Ben could have had an itch for that. But mainly he was that way, careful and concerned. He had in mind what we all felt, that just as absolutely anything could be done by Mayfred, so could absolutely anything happen to her. He also knew what we all knew, that if the Colosseum started falling on her, Jamie would leap bodily under the rocks.

At two a.m. it was too much for me to think about. I went to bed and was so exhausted I didn't even hear Mayfred leave.

I woke up about ten with a low tapping on my door. It was Eric. "Is this the sleep of the just?" he asked me as I opened the door. The air in the corridor was fresh: it must have rained in the night. No one was about. All the guests, I supposed, were well out into the day's routine, seeing what next tour was on the list. On a trip you were always planning something. Ben planned for us. He kept a little notebook.

Standing in my doorway alone with Eric, in a loose robe with a cool morning breeze and my hair not even combed, I suddenly laughed. Eric laughed, too. "I'm glad they're gone," he said, and looked past my shoulder.

I dressed and went out with him for some breakfast, cappuccino and croissants at a café in the Signoria. We didn't talk much. It was terrible, in the sense of the Mason Skinner

Marshall and Phillips sense of family, even to think you were glad they were gone, let alone say it. I took Eric's silence as one of his ironies, what he was best at. He would say, for instance, if you were discussing somebody's problem that wouldn't ever have any solution, "It's time somebody died." There wasn't much to say after that. Another time, when his daddy got into a rage with a next-door neighbor over their property line, Eric said, "You'd better marry her." Once he put things in an extreme light, nobody could talk about them anymore. Saying "I'm glad they're gone" was like that.

But it was a break. I thought of the way I'd been seeing them. How Jamie's becoming had been impressing me, every day more. How Mayfred was a kind of spirit, grown bigger than life. How Ben's dominance now seemed not worrisome but princely, his heritage. We were into a Renaissance of ourselves, I wanted to say, but was afraid they wouldn't see it the way I did. Only Eric had eluded me. What was he becoming? For once he didn't have to discuss Poe's idea of women, or the Southern code of honor, or Henry James's views of France and England.

As for me, I was, at least, sure that my style had changed. I had bought my little linen blouses and loose skirts, my sandals and braided silver bracelets. "That's great on you!" Mayfred had cried. "Now try this one!" On the streets, Italians passed me too close not to be noticed; they murmured musically in my ear, saying I didn't know just what; waiters leaned on my shoulder to describe dishes of the day.

Eric and I wandered across the river, following narrow streets lined with great stone palaces, seeing them open into small piazzas whose names were not well known. We had lunch in a friendly place with a curtain of thin twisted metal sticks in the open door, an amber-colored dog lying on the marble floor near the serving table. We ordered favorite things without looking at the menu. We drank white wine. "This is fun," I suddenly said. He turned to me. Out of his private distance, he seemed to be looking at me. "I think so, too."

He suddenly switched on to me, like somebody searching and finding with the lens of a camera. He began to ask me things. What did you think of that, Ella Mason? What about this, Ella Mason? Ella Mason, did you think Ben was right when he said . . . ? I could hardly swing on to what was being asked of me, thick and fast. But he seemed to like my answers, actually to listen. Not that all those years I'd been dumb as a stone. I had prattled quite a lot. It's just that they never treated me one to one, the way Eric was doing now. We talked for nearly an hour, then, with no one left in the restaurant but us, stopped as suddenly as we'd started. Eric said, "That's a pretty dress."

The sun was strong outside. The dog was asleep near the door. Even the one remaining waiter was drowsing on his feet. It was the shutting-up time for everything and we went out into the streets blanked out with metal shutters. We hugged the shady side and went single-file back to home base, as we'd come to call it, wherever we stayed.

A Vespa snarled by and I stepped into a cool courtyard to avoid it. I found myself in a large, yawning mouth, mysterious as a cave, shadowy, with the trickling sound of a fountain and the glimmer in the depths of water running through ferns and moss. Along the interior of the street wall, fragments of ancient sculpture, found, I guess, when they'd built the palazzo, had been set into the masonry. One was a horse, neck and shoulder, another an arm holding a shield, and a third at about my height the profile of a woman, a nymph or some such. Eric stopped to look at each, for as Ben said, Eric loved everything there, and then he said, "Come here, Ella Mason." I stood where he wanted, by the little sculptured relief, and he took my face and turned it to look at it closer; then with a strong hand (I remembered tennis), he pressed my face against the stone face and held it for a moment. The stone bit into my flesh and that was the first time that Eric, bending deliberately to do so, kissed me on the mouth. He had held one side of me against the wall, so that I couldn't raise my arm to him, and the other arm was pinned down by his elbow; the hand that pressed my face into the stone was that one, so that I couldn't move closer to him, as I wanted to do, and when he dropped away suddenly, turned on his heel and walked rapidly away, I could only hasten to follow, my voice gone, my pulses all throbbing together. I remember my anger, the old dreams about him and Ben stirred to life again, thinking, *If he thinks he can just walk away,* and knowing with anger, too, *It's got to be now,* as if in the walled land of kinship, thicker in our illustrious connection than any fortress in Europe, a door had cracked open at last. Eric, Eric, Eric. I'm always seeing your retreating heels, how they looked angry; but why? It was worth coming for, after thirty years, to ask that.

"That day you kissed me in the street, the first time," I asked him. Night on the terrace; a bottle of Chianti between our chairs. "You walked away. Were you angry? Your heels looked angry. I can see them still."

"The trip in the first place," he said, "it had to do with you, partly. Maybe you didn't understand that. We were outward bound, leaving you, a sister in a sense. We'd talked about it."

"I'd adored you so," I said. "I think I was less than a sister, more like a dog."

"For a little while you weren't either one." He found my hand in the dark. "It was a wonderful little while."

Memories: Eric in the empty corridor of the *pensione.* How Italy folds up and goes to sleep from two to four. His not looking back for me, going straight to his door. The door closing, but no key turning and me turning the door handle and stepping in. And he at the window already with his back to me and how he heard the sliding latch on the door—I slid it with my hands behind me—heard it click shut, and turned. His face and mine, what we knew. Betraying Ben.

: Walking by the Arno, watching a white-and-green scull stroking by into the twilight, the rower a boy or girl in white and green, growing dimmer to the rhythm of the long oars, vanishing into arrow shape, then pencil thickness, then movement without substance, on . . .

: A trek the next afternoon through twisted streets to a famous chapel. Sitting quiet in a cloister, drinking in the symmetry, the silence. Holding hands. "D for Donatello," said Eric. "D for Della Robbia," I said. "M for Michelangelo," he continued. "M for Medici." "L for Leonardo." "I can't think of an L," I gave up. "Lumbago. There's an old master." "Worse than Jamie." We were always going home again.

: Running into the manager of the *pensione* one morning in the corridor. He'd solemnly bowed to us and kissed my hand. *"Bella ragazza,"* he remarked. "The way life ought to be," said Eric. I thought we might be free forever, but from what?

At the train station waiting the departure we were supposed to take for Rome, "Why do we have to go?" I pleaded. "Why can't we just stay here?"

"Use your common sense, Ella Mason."

"I don't have any."

He squeezed my shoulder. "We'll get by all right," he said. "That is, if you don't let on."

I promised not to. Rather languidly I watched the landscape slide past as we glided south. I would obey Eric, I thought, for always. "Once I wrote a love letter to you," I said. "I wrote it at night by candlelight at home one summer. I tore it up."

"You told me that," he recalled, "but you said you couldn't remember if it was to me or Ben."

"I just remembered," I said. "It was you . . ."

"Why did we ever leave?" I asked Eric, in the dead of night, a blackness now. "Why did we ever decide we had to go to Rome?"

"I didn't think of it as even a choice," he said. "But at that point, how could I know what was there, ahead?"

We got off the train feeling small—at least, I did. Ben was standing there, looking around him, tall, searching for us, then seeing. But no Jamie. Something to ask. I wondered if he'd gone back with Mayfred. "No, he's running around Rome." The big, smooth station, echoing, open to the warm day. "Hundreds of churches," Ben went on. "Millions. He's checking them off." He helped us in a taxi with the skill of somebody who'd lived in Rome for ten years, and gave the address. "He's got to do something now that Mayfred's gone. It's getting like something he might take seriously, is all. Finding out what Catholics believe. He's either losing all his money, or falling in love, or getting religion."

"He didn't lose any money," said Eric. "He made some."

"Well, it's the same thing," said Ben, always right and not wanting to argue with us. He seemed a lot older than the two of us, at least to me. Ben was tall.

We had mail in Rome; Ben brought it to the table that night. I read Mama's aloud to them: "When I think of you children over there, I count you all like my own chickens out in the yard, thinking I've got to go out in the dark and make sure the gate's locked because not a one ought to get out of there. To me, you're all my own, and thinking of chickens is my way of saying prayers for you to be safe at home again."

"You'd think we were off in a war," said Eric.

"It's a bold metaphor," said Ben, pouring wine for us, "but that never stopped Cousin Charlotte."

I wanted to giggle at Mama, as I usually did, but instead my eyes filled with tears, surprising me, and a minute more and I would have dared to snap at Ben. But Eric, who had got some mail, too, abruptly got up and left the table. I almost ran after him, but intent on what I'd promised about not letting on to Ben, I stayed and finished dinner. He had been pale, white. Ben thought he might be sick. He didn't return. We didn't know.

Jamie and Ben finally went to bed. "He'll come back when he wants to," said Ben.

I waited till their door had closed, and then, possessed, I crept out to the front desk. "Signor Mason," I said, "the one with the *capelli leggero*—" My Italian came from the dictionary straight to the listener. I found out later I had said that Eric's hair didn't weigh much. Still, they understood. He had taken a room, someone who spoke English explained. He wanted to be alone. I said he might be sick, and I guess they could read my face because I was guided by a porter, in a blue working jacket and cloth shoes, into a labyrinth. Italian buildings, I knew by now, are constructed like dreams. There are passages departing from central hallways, stairs that twist back upon themselves, dark silent doors. My guide stopped before one. *"Ecco,"* he said and left. I knocked softly, and the door eventually cracked open. "Oh, it's you." "Eric. Are you all right? I didn't know . . ."

He opened the door a little wider. "Ella Mason—" he began. Maybe he was sick. I caught his arm. The whole intensity of my young life in that moment shook free of everything but Eric. It was as though I'd traveled miles to find him. I came inside and we kissed and then I was sitting apart from him on the edge of the bed and he in a chair, and a letter, official-looking, the top of the envelope torn open in a jagged line, lay on a high black-marble-topped table with bowed legs, between us. He said to read it and I did, and put it back where I found it.

It said that Eric had failed his law exams. That in view of the family connection with the university (his father had gone there and some cousin was head of the board of trustees) a special meeting had been held to grant his repeating the term's work so as to graduate in the fall, but the evidences of his negligence were too numerous and the vote had gone against it. I remember saying something like "Anybody can fail exams . . ." as I knew people who had, but knew also that those people weren't "us," not one of our class or connection, not kin to the brilliant Ben, or nephew of a governor, or descended from a great Civil War general.

"All year long," he said, "I've been acting like a fool, as if I expected to get by. This last semester especially. It all seemed too easy. It is easy. It's easy and boring. I was fencing blindfold with somebody so far beneath me it wasn't worth the trouble to look at him. The only way to keep the interest up was to see how close I could come without damage. Well, I ran right into it, head on. God, does it serve me right. I'd read books Ben was reading, follow his interests, instead of boning over law. But I wanted the degree. Hot damn, I wanted it!"

"Another school," I said. "You can transfer credits and start over."

"This won't go away."

"Everybody loves you," I faltered, adding, "Especially me."

He almost laughed, at my youngness, I guess, but then said, "Ella Mason," as gently as feathers falling, and came to hold me awhile, but not like before, the way we'd been. We sat down on the bed and then fell back on it and I could hear his heart's steady thumping under his shirt. But it wasn't the beat of a lover's heart just then; it was more like the echo of a distant bell or the near march of a clock; and I fell to looking over his shoulder.

It was a curious room, one I guess they wouldn't have rented to anybody if Rome hadn't been, as they told us, so full. The shutters outside were closed on something that suggested more of a courtyard than the outside, as no streak or glimmer of light came through, and the bed was huge, with a great dark tall rectangle of a headboard and a footboard only slightly lower. There were brass sconces set ornamentally around the moldings, looking down, cupids and fauns and smiling goat faces, with bulbs concealed in them, though the only light came from the one dim lamp on the bedside table. There were heavy, dark engravings of Rome—by Piranesi or somebody like that—the avenues, the monuments, the river. And one panel of small pictures in a series showed some familiar scenes in Florence.

My thoughts, unable to reach Eric's, kept wandering off tourist-fashion among the myth faces peeking from the sconces, laughing down, among the walks of Rome—the arched bridge over the Tiber where life-size angels stood poised; the rise of the Palatine, mysterious among trees; the horseman on the Campidoglio, his hand outstretched; and Florence, beckoning still. I couldn't keep my mind at any one set with all such around me, and Eric, besides, had gone back to the table and was writing a letter on hotel stationery. When my caught breath turned to a little cry, he looked up and said, "It's my problem, Ella Mason. Just let me handle it." He came to stand by me, and pressed my head against him, then lifted my face by the chin. "Don't go talking about it. Promise." I promised.

I wandered back through the labyrinth, thinking I'd be lost in there forever like a Poe lady. Damn Ben, I thought, he's too above it all for anybody to fall in love or fail an examination. I'm better off lost, at this rate. So thinking, I turned a corner and stepped out into the hotel lobby.

It was Jamie's and Ben's assumption that Eric had picked up some girl and gone home with her. I never told them better. Let them think that.

"Your Mama wrote you a letter about some chickens once, how she counted children like counting chickens," Eric said, thirty years later. "Do you remember that?"

We fell to remembering Mama. "There's nobody like her,"

I said. "She has long talks with Papa. They started a year or so after he died. I wish I could talk to him."

"What would you say?"

"I'd ask him to look up Howard. See'f he's doing all right."

"Your husband?" Eric wasn't that sure of the name.

I guess joking about your husband's death isn't quite the thing. I met Howard on a trip to Texas after we got home from abroad. I was visiting my roommate. Whatever else Eric did for me, our time together had made me ready for more. I pined for him alone, but what I looked was ripe and ready for practically anybody. So Howard said. He was a widower with a Texas-size fortune. When he said I looked like a good breeder, I didn't even get mad. That's how he knew I'd do. Still, it took awhile. I kept wanting Eric, wanting my old dream: my brilliant cousins, princely, cavalier.

Howard and I had two sons, in their twenties now. Howard got killed in a jeep accident out on his cattle ranch. Don't think I didn't get married again, to a wild California boy ten years younger. It lasted six months exactly.

"What about that other one?" Eric asked me. "Number two."

I had gotten the divorce papers the same day they called to say Howard's tombstone had arrived. "Well, you know, Eric, I always was a little bit crazy."

"You thought he was cute."

"I guess so."

"You and I," said Eric, smooth as silk into the deep, silent darkness that now was ours—even the towers seemed to have folded up and gone home—"we never worked it out, did we?"

"I never knew if you really wanted to. I did, God knows. I wouldn't marry Howard for over a year because of you."

"I stayed undecided about everything. One thing that's not is a marrying frame of mind."

"Then you left for Europe."

"I felt I'd missed the boat for everywhere else. War service, then that law school thing. It was too late for me. And nothing was of interest. I could move but not with much conviction. I felt for you—maybe more than you know—but you were moving on already. You know, Ella Mason, you never are still."

"But you could have told me that!"

"I think I did, one way or another. You sat still and fidgeted." He laughed.

It's true that energy is my middle name.

The lights along the river were dim and so little was moving past by now they seemed fixed and distant, stars from some long-dead galaxy maybe. I think I slept. Then I heard Eric.

"I think back so often to the five of us—you and Ben, Jamie and Mayfred and me. There was something I could never get out of my mind. You remember when we were planning everything about Europe Europe Europe, before we left, and you'd all come over to my house and we'd sit out on the side porch, listening to Ben mainly but with Jamie asking some questions, like 'Do they have bathtubs like us?' Remember that? You would snuggle down in one of those canvas chairs like a sling, and Ben was in the big armchair—Daddy's—and Jamie sort of sprawled around on the couch among the travel folders, when we heard the front gate scrape on the sidewalk and heard the way it would clatter when it closed. A warm night and the streetlight filtering in patterns through the trees and shrubs and a smell of honeysuckle from where it was all baled up on the yard fence, and a Cape jessamine outside. I remember that, too—white flowers in among the leaves. And steps on the walk. They stopped, then they walked again, and Ben got up (I should have) and unlatched the screen. If you didn't latch the screen it wouldn't shut. Mayfred came in. Jamie said, 'Why'd you stop on the walk, Mayfred?' She said, 'There was this toad-frog. I almost stepped on him.' Then she was among us, walking in, one of us. I was sitting back in the corner, watching, and I felt, If I live to be a thousand, I'll never feel more love than I do this minute. Love of these, my blood, and this place, here. I could close my eyes for years and hear the gate scrape, the steps pause, the door latch and unlatch, hear her say, 'There was this toad-frog . . .' I would want literally to embrace that one minute, hold it forever."

"But you're not there," I said, into the dark. "You're here. Where we were. You chose it."

"There's no denying that" was all he answered.

We had sailed from Naples, a sad day under mist, with Vesuvius hardly visible and damp clinging to everything—the end of summer. We couldn't even make out the outlines of the ship, an Italian Line monster from those days called the *Independence.* It towered white over us and we tunneled in. The crossing was rainy and drab. Crossed emotions played amongst us, while Ben, noble and aware, tried to be our mast. He read aloud to us, discussed, joked, tried to get our attention.

Jamie wanted to argue about Catholicism. It didn't suit Ben for him to drift that way. Ben was headed toward Anglican belief: that's what his Sylvia was, not to mention T. S. Eliot. But in Rome Jamie had met an American Jesuit from Indiana and chummed around with him; they'd even gone to the beach. "You're wrong about that," I heard him tell Ben. "I'm going to prove it by Father Rogers when we get home."

I worried about Eric; I longed for Eric; I strolled the decks and stood by Eric at the rail. He looked with gray eyes out at a gray sea. He said: "You know, Ella Mason, I don't give a damn if Jamie joins the Catholic Church or not." "Me either," I agreed. We kissed in the dark beneath the lifeboats, and made love once in the cabin while Ben and Jamie were at the movies, but in a furtive way, as if the grown people were at church. Ben read aloud to us from a book on Hadrian's Villa, where we'd all been. There was a half day of sun.

I went to the pool to swim, and up came Jamie, out of the water. He was skinny, string beans and spaghetti. "Ella Mason," he said, in his dark croak of a voice, "I'll never be the same again." I was tired of all of them, even Jamie. "Then gain some weight," I snapped, and went pretty off the diving board.

Ben knew about the law school thing. The first day out, coming from the writing lounge, I saw Eric and Ben standing together in a corner of an enclosed deck. Ben had a letter in his hand, and just from one glance I recognized the stationery of the hotel where we'd stayed in Rome and knew it was the letter Eric had been writing. I heard Ben: "You say it's not important, but I know it is—I knew that last Christmas." And Eric, "Think what you like, it's not to me." And Ben, "What you feel about it, that's not what matters. There's a right way of looking at it. Only to make you see it." And Eric, "You'd better give up; you never will."

What kept me in my tracks was something multiple, yet single, the way a number can contain powers and elements that have gone into its making, and can be unfolded, opened up, nearly forever. Ambition and why some had it, success and failure and what the difference was, and why you had to notice it at all. These matters, back and forth across the net, were what was going on.

What had stopped me in the first place, though, and chilled me, was that they sounded angry. I knew they had quarreled last Christmas; was this why? It must have been. Ben's anger was attack, and Eric's self-defense, defiance. Hadn't they always been like brothers? Yes, and they were standing so, intent, a little apart, in hot debate, like two officers locked in different plans of attack at dawn, stubbornly held to the point of fury. Ben's position, based on rightness, classical and firm. Enforced by what he was. And Eric's wrong, except in and for himself, for holding on to himself. How to defend that? He couldn't, but he did. And equally. They were just looking up and seeing me, and nervous at my intrusion I stepped across the high shipboard sill to the deck, missed clearing it and fell sprawling. "Oh, Ella Mason!" they cried at once and picked me up, the way they always had.

One more thing I remember from that ship. It was Ben, finding me one night after dinner alone in the lounge. Everyone was below: we were docking in the morning. He sat down and lighted his pipe. "It's all passed so fast, don't you think?" he said. There was such a jumble in my mind still, I didn't answer. All I could hear was Eric saying, after we'd made love: "It's got to stop now; I've got to find some shape to things. There was promise, promises. You've got to see we're saying they're worthless, that nothing matters." What did matter to me, except Eric? "I wish I'd never come," I burst out at Ben, childish, hurting him, I guess. How much did Ben know? He never said. He came close and put his arm around me. "You're the sister I never had," he said. "I hope you change your mind about it." I said I was sorry and snuffled awhile, into his shoulder. When I looked up, I saw his love. So maybe he did know, and forgave us. He kissed my forehead.

At the New York pier, who should show up but Mayfred.

She was crisp in black and white, her long blond hair windshaken, her laughter a wholesome joy. "Y'all look just terrible," she told us with a friendly giggle, and as usual made us straighten up, tuck our tummies in, and look like quality. Jamie forgot religion, and Eric quit worrying over a missing bag, and Ben said, "Well, look who's here!" "How's Donald?" I asked her. I figured he was either all right or dead. The first was true. They didn't have to do a brain tumor operation; all he'd had was a pinched nerve at the base of his cortex. "What's a cortex?" Jamie asked. "It sounds too personal to inquire," said Eric, and right then they brought him his bag.

On the train home, Mayfred rode backward in our large

drawing-room compartment (courtesy of Donald Bailey) and the landscape, getting more Southern every minute, went rocketing past. "You can't guess how I spent my time when Donald was in the hospital. Nothing to do but sit."

"Working crossword puzzles," said Jamie.

"Crocheting," said Eric, provoking a laugh.

"Reading *Vogue,*" said Ben.

"All wrong! I read Edgar Allan Poe! What's more, I memorized that poem! That one Ben wrote on. You know? That 'Ulalume'!"

Everybody laughed but Ben, and Mayfred was laughing, too, her grand girlish sputters, innocent as sun and water, her beautiful large white teeth, even as a cover girl's. Ben, courteously at the end of the sofa, smiled faintly. It was best not to believe this was true.

> *" 'The skies they were ashen and sober;*
> *The leaves they were crispéd and sere—*
> *The leaves they were withering and sere;*
> *It was the night in the lonesome October*
> *Of my most immemorial year . . .' "*

"By God, she's done it," said Ben.

At that point Jamie and I began to laugh, and Eric, who had at first looked quizzical, started laughing, too. Ben said, "Oh, cut it out, Mayfred," but she said, "No, sir, I'm not! I *did* all that. I know *every* word! Just wait, I'll show you." She went right on, full speed, to the "ghoul-haunted woodland of Weir."

Back as straight as a ramrod, Ben left the compartment. Mayfred stopped. An hour later, when he came back, she started again. But it wasn't till she got to Psyche "uplifting her finger" (Mayfred lifted hers), saying, "Oh, fly!—let us fly!—for we must," and all that about the "tremulous light," the "crystalline light," etc., that Ben gave up and joined in the general merriment. She actually did know it, every word. He followed along openmouthed through "Astarte" and "Sybillic," and murmured, "Oh, my God," when she got to

> *". . . 'Ulalume—Ulalume—*
> *'Tis the vault of thy lost Ulalume!' "*

because she let go in a wail like a hound's bugle and the conductor, who was passing, looked in to see if we were all right.

We rolled into Chattanooga in the best of humor and filed off the train into the waiting arms of my parents, Eric's parents, and selected members from Ben's and Jamie's families. There was nobody from Mayfred's but they'd sent word. They all kept checking us over, as though we might need washing, or might have gotten scarred some way. "Just promise me one thing!" Mama kept saying, just about to cry. "Don't y'all ever go away again, you hear? Not all of you! Just promise you won't do it! Promise me right now!"

I guess we must have promised, the way she was begging us to.

Ben married his Sylvia, with her pedigree and family estate in Connecticut. He's a big professor, lecturing in literature, up East. Jamie married a Catholic girl from West Virginia. He works in her father's firm and has sired a happy lot of kids. Mayfred went to New York after she left Donald and works for a big fashion house. She's been in and out of marriages, from time to time.

And Eric and I are sitting holding hands on a terrace in far-off Italy. Midnight struck long ago, and we know it. We are sitting there, talking, in the pitch black dark.

JACK OF DIAMONDS

One April afternoon, Central Park, right across the street, turned green all at once. It was a green toned with gold and seemed less a color of leaves than a stained cloud settled down to stay. Rosalind brought her bird book out on the terrace and turned her face up to seek out something besides pigeons. She arched, to hang her long hair backward over the terrace railing, soaking in sunlight while the starlings whirled by.

The phone rang, and she went inside.

"I just knew you'd be there, Rosie," her father said. "What a gorgeous day. Going to get hotter. You know what I'm thinking about? Lake George."

"Let's go right now," Rosalind said.

The cottage was at Bolton Landing. Its balconies were built out over the water. You walked down steps and right off into the lake, or into the boat. In a lofty beamed living room, shadows of water played against the walls and ceiling. There was fine lake air, and chill pure evenings . . .

The intercom sounded. "Gristede's, Daddy. They're buzzing."

Was it being in the theater that made her father, whenever

another call came, exert himself to get more into the first? "Let's think about getting up there, Rosie. Summer's too short as it is. You ask Eva when she comes in. Warm her up to it. We'll make our pitch this evening. She's never even seen it . . . can you beat that?"

"I'm not sure she'll even like it," Rosalind said.

"Won't like it? It's hardly camping out. Of course she'll love it. Get it going, Rosie baby. I'm aiming for home by seven."

The grocer's son who brought the order up wore jeans just like Rosalind's. "It's getting hot," he remarked. "It's about melted my ass off."

"Let's see if you brought everything." She had tried to give up presiding over the food after her father remarried, but when her stepmother turned out not to care much about what happened in the kitchen, she had cautiously gone back to seeing about things.

"If I forgot, I'll get it. But if you think of something—"

"I know, I'll come myself. You think you got news?"

They were old friends. They sassed each other. His name was Luis—Puerto Rican.

It was after the door to the service entrance closed with its hollow echo, and was bolted, and the service elevator had risen, opened, and closed on Luis, that Rosalind felt the changed quality in things, a new direction, like the tilt of an airliner's wing. She went to the terrace and found the park's greenness surer of itself than ever. She picked up her book and went inside. A boy at school, seeing her draw birds, had given it to her. She stored it with her special treasures.

Closing the drawer, she jerked her head straight, encountering her own wide blue gaze in her bedroom mirror. From the entrance hall, a door was closing. She gathered up a pack of cards spread out for solitaire and slid them into a gilded box. She whacked at her long brown hair with a brush; then she went out. It was Eva.

Rosalind Jennings's stepmother had short, raven-black glossy hair, a full red mouth, jetty brows and lashes. Shortsighted, she handled the problem in the most open way, by wearing great round glasses trimmed in tortoiseshell. All through the winter—a winter Rosalind would always remember as The Stepmother: Year I—Eva had gone around the apartment in gold wedge-heeled slippers, pink slacks, and a black chiffon blouse. Noiseless on the wall-to-wall carpets, the slippers slapped faintly against stockings or flesh when she walked—spaced, intimate ticks of sound. "Let's face it, Rosie," her father said, when Eva went off to the kitchen for a fresh drink as he tossed in his blackjack hand. "She's a sexy dame."

Sexy or not, she was kind to Rosalind. "I wouldn't have married anybody you didn't like," her father told her. "That child's got *the* most heavenly eyes," she'd overheard Eva say.

Arriving now, having triple-locked the apartment door, Eva set the inevitable Saks parcels down on the foyer table and dumped her jersey jacket off her arm onto the chair with a gasp of relief. "It's turned so hot!" Rosalind followed her to the kitchen, where she poured orange juice and soda over ice. Her nails were firm, hard, perfectly painted. They resembled, to Rosalind, ten small creatures who had ranked themselves on this stage of fingertips. Often they ticked off a pile of poker chips from top to bottom, red and white, as Eva pondered. "Stay . . ." or "Call . . ." or "I'm out . . ." then, "Oh, damn you, Nat . . . that's twice in a row."

"I've just been talking on the phone to Daddy," Rosalind said. "I've got to warn you. He's thinking of the cottage."

"Up there in Vermont?"

"It's in New York, on Lake George. Mother got it from her folks. You know, they lived in Albany. The thing is, Daddy's always loved it. He's hoping you will too, I think."

Eva finished her orange juice. Turning to rinse the glass in the sink, she wafted out perfume and perspiration. "It's a little far for a summer place. . . . But if it's what you and Nat like, why, then . . ." She affectionately pushed a dark strand of Rosalind's hair back behind her ear. Her fingers were chilly from the glass. "I'm yours to command." Her smile, intimate and confident, seemed to repeat its red picture on every kitchen object.

Daughter and stepmother had got a lot chummier in the six months since her father had married. At first, Rosalind was always wondering what they thought of her. For here was a new "they," like a whole new being. She had heard, for instance, right after the return from the Nassau honeymoon:

Eva: "I want to be sure and leave her room just the way it is."

Nat: "I think that's right. Change is up to her."

But Rosalind could not stop her angry thought: *You'd just better try touching my room!* Her mother had always chosen her decor, always the rose motif, roses in the wallpaper and deeper rose valances and matching draperies. This was a romantic theme with her parents, accounting for her name. Her father would warble "Sweet Rosie O'Grady" while downing his whiskey. He would waltz his little girl around the room. She'd learned to dance before she could walk, she thought.

"Daddy sets the music together with what's happening on the stage. He gets the dancers and actors to carry out the music. That's different from composing or writing lyrics." So Rosalind would explain to new friends at school, every year. Now she'd go off to some other school next fall, still ready with her lifelong lines. "You must have heard of some of his shows. Remember So-and-So, and then there was . . ." Watching their impressionable faces form their cries. "We've got the records of that!" "Was your mother an actress?" "My stepmother used to be an actress—nobody you'd know about. My mother died. She wasn't ever in the theater. She studied art history at Vassar." Yes, and married the assistant manager of his family firm: Jennings' Finest Woolen Imports; he did not do well. Back to his first love, theater. From college on they thought they'd never get him out of it, and they were right. Some purchase he had chosen in West Germany turned out to be polyester, sixty percent. "I had a will to fail," Nat Jennings would shrug, when he thought about it. "If your heart's not in something, you can't succeed" was her mother's reasoning, clinging to her own sort of knowing, which had to do with the things you picked, felt about, what went where. Now here was another woman with other thoughts about the same thing. She'd better not touch my room, thought Rosalind, or I'll . . . what? Trip her in the hallway, hide her glasses, throw the keys out the window?

"What are you giggling at, Rosie?"

Well might they ask, just back from Nassau at a time of falling leaves. "I'm wondering what to do with this leg of lamb. It's too long and skinny."

"Broil it like a great big chop." Still honeymooning, they'd be holding hands, she bet, on the living-room sofa.

"Just you leave my room alone," she sang out to this new Them. "Or I won't cook for you!"

"Atta girl, Rosie!"

Now, six months later in the balmy early evening with windows wide open, they were saying it again. Daddy had come in, hardly even an hour later than he said, and there was the big conversation, starting with cocktails, lasting through dinner, all about Lake George and how to get there, where to start, but all totally impossible until day after tomorrow at the soonest.

"One of the few unpolluted lakes left!" Daddy enthused to Eva. It was true. If you dropped anything from the boat into the water, your mother would call from the balcony, "It's right down there, darling," and you'd see it as plainly as if it lay in sunlight at your feet and you could reach down for it instead of diving. The caretaker they'd had for years, Mr.

Thibodeau, reported to them from time to time. Everything was all right, said Mr. Thibodeau. He had about fifteen houses on his list, for watching over, especially during the long winters. He was good. They'd left the cottage empty for two summers, and it was still all right. She remembered the last time they were there, June three years back. She and Daddy were staying while Mother drove back to New York, planning to see Aunt Mildred from Denver before she put out for the West again. "What a nuisance she can't come here!" Mother had said. "It's going to be sticky as anything in town, and when I think of that Thruway!"

"Say you've got food poisoning," said Daddy. "Make something up."

"But Nat! Can't you understand? I really *do* want to see Mildred!" It was Mother's little cry that still sounded in Rosalind's head. "Whatever you do, please don't go to the apartment," Daddy said. He hadn't washed dishes for a week; he'd be ashamed for an in-law to have an even lower opinion of him, though he thought it wasn't possible. "It's a long drive," her mother pondered. "Take the Taconic, it's cooler." "Should I spend one night or two?"

Her mother was killed on the Taconic Parkway the next day by a man coming out of a crossover. There must have been a moment of terrible disbelief when she saw that he was actually going to cross in front of her. Wasn't he looking, didn't he see? They would never know. He died in the ambulance. She was killed at once.

Rosalind and her father, before they left, had packed all her mother's clothing and personal things, but that was all they'd had the heart for. The rest they walked off and left, just so. "Next summer," they had said, as the weeks wore on and still they'd made no move. The next summer came, and still they did not stir. One day they said, "Next summer." Mr. Thibodeau said not to worry, everything was fine. So the Navaho rugs were safe, and all the pottery, the copper and brass, the racked pewter. The books would all be lined in place on the shelves, the music in the Victorian music rack just as it had been left, Schumann's "Carnaval" (she could see it still) on top. And if everything was really fine, the canoe would be dry, though dusty and full of spiderwebs, suspended out in the boathouse, and the roof must be holding firm and dry, as Mr. Thibodeau would have reported any leak immediately. All that had happened, he said, was that the steps into the water had to have new uprights, the bottom two replaced, and that the eaves on the northeast corner had broken from a falling limb and been repaired.

Mention of the fallen limb recalled the storms. Rosalind remembered them blamming away while she and her mother huddled back of the stairway, feeling aimed at by the thunderbolts; or if Daddy was there, they'd sing by candlelight while he played the piano. He dared the thunder by imitating it in the lower bass. . . .

"Atta girl, Rosie."

She had just said she wasn't afraid to go up there alone tomorrow, take the bus or train, and consult with Mr. Thibodeau. The Thibodeaus had long ago taken a fancy to Rosalind; a French Canadian, Mrs. Thibodeau had taught her some French songs, and fed her on *tourtière* and beans.

"That would be wonderful," said Eva.

"I just can't let her do it," Nat said.

"I can stay at Howard Johnson's. After all, I'm seventeen."

While she begged, her father looked at her steadily from the end of the table, finishing coffee. "I'll telephone the Thibodeaus," he finally said. "One thing you aren't to do is stay in the house alone. Howard Johnson's is okay. We'll get you a room there." Then, because he knew what the house had meant and wanted to let her know it, he took her shoulder (Eva not being present) and squeezed it, his eyes looking deep into hers, and Irish tears rising moistly. "Life goes on, Rosie," he whispered. "It has to."

She remembered all that, riding the bus. But it was for some unspoken reason that he had wanted her to go. And she knew that it was right for her to do it, not only to see about things. It was an important journey. For both of them? Yes, for them both.

Mr. Thibodeau himself met her bus, driving up to Lake George Village.

"Not many people yet," he said. "We had a good many on the weekend, out to enjoy the sun. Starting a baseball team up here. The piers took a beating back in the winter. Not enough ice and too much wind. How's your daddy?"

"He's fine. He wants to come back here now."

"You like your new mother? Shouldn't ask. Just curious."

"She's nice," said Rosalind.

"Hard to be a match for the first one."

Rosalind did not answer. She had a quietly aware way of closing her mouth when she did not care to reply.

"Pretty?" pursued Mr. Thibodeau. Not only the caretaker, Mr. Thibodeau was also a neighbor. He lived between the property and the road. You had to be nice to the Thibodeaus; so much depended on them.

"Yes, she's awfully pretty. She was an actress. She had just a little part in the cast of the show he worked with last year."

"That's how they met, was it?"

To Rosalind, it seemed that Eva had just showed up one evening in her father's conversation at dinner. "There's somebody I want you to meet, Rosie. She's—well, she's a she. I've seen her once or twice. I think you'll like her. But if you don't, we'll scratch her, Rosie. That's a promise."

"Here's a list, Mr. Thibodeau," she said. "All the things Daddy wants done are on it. Telephone, plumbing, electricity . . . maybe Mrs. Thibodeau can come in and clean. I've got to check the linens for mildew. Then go through the canned stuff and make a grocery list."

"We got a new supermarket since you stopped coming, know that?"

"I bet."

"We'll go tomorrow. I'll take you."

The wood-lined road had been broken into over and over on the lake side, the other side, too, by new motels. Signs about pools, TV, vacancy came rudely up and at them, until, swinging left, they entered woods again and drew near the cutoff to the narrow, winding drive among the pines. "Thibodeau" the mailbox read in strong, irregular letters, and by its side a piece of weathered plywood nailed to the fence post said "Jennings," painted freshly over the ghost of old lettering beneath.

She bounced along with Mr. Thibodeau, who, his black hair grayed over, still had his same beaked nose, which in her mind gave him his Frenchness and his foreignness. Branches slapped the car window. The tires squished through ruts felted with fallout from the woods. They reached the final bend. "Stop," said Rosalind, for something white that gave out a sound like dry bones breaking had passed beneath the wheels. She jumped out. It was only birch branches, half rotted. "I'll go alone." She ran ahead of his station wagon, over pine needles and through the fallen leaves of two autumns, which slowed her motion until she felt the way she did in dreams.

The cottage was made of natural wood, no shiny lacquer covering it; boughs around it, pine and oak, pressed down like protective arms. The reach of the walls was laced over with undergrowth, so that the house at first glance looked small as a hut, not much wider than the door. Running there, Rosalind tried the knob with the confidence of a child running to her mother, only to find it locked, naturally; then with a child's abandon, she flung out her arms against the paneling, hearing her heart thump on the wood until Mr. Thibodeau gently detached her little by little as though she had got stuck there.

"Now there . . . now there . . . just let me get hold of this key." He had a huge wire ring for his keys, labels attached to each. His clientele. *"Des clients, vous en avez beaucoup,"* Rosalind had once said to him as she was starting French in school. But Mr. Thibodeau was unregretfully far from his Quebec origins. His family had come there from northern Vermont to get a milder climate. Lake George was a sun trap, a village sliding off the Adirondacks toward the lake, facing a daylong exposure.

The key ground in the lock. Mr. Thibodeau kicked the base of the door, and the hinges whined. He let her enter alone, going tactfully back to his station wagon for nothing at all. He gave her time to wander before he followed her.

She would have had to come someday, Rosalind thought, one foot following the other, moving forward: the someday was this one. It wasn't as if anything had actually "happened" there. The door frame that opened from the entrance hall into the living room did not face the front door but was about ten feet from it to the left. Thus the full scope of the high, shadowy room, which was the real heart of the cottage, opened all at once to the person entering. Suddenly, there was an interior world. The broad windows opposite, peaked in an irregular triangle at the top, like something in a modernistic church, opened onto the lake, and from the water a rippling light, muted by shade, played constantly on the high-beamed ceiling. Two large handwoven Indian rugs covered the central area of floor; on a table before the windows, a huge pot of brown-and-beige pottery was displayed, filled with money plant that had grown dusty and ragged. There were coarse-fibered curtains in off-white monk's cloth, now dragging askew, chair coverings in heavy fabric, orange-and-white cushions, and the piano, probably so out of tune now with the damp it would never sound right, which sat closed and silent in the corner. An open stairway, more like a ladder than a stair, rose to the upper-floor balcony, with bedrooms in the wing.

"We're going to fall and break our silly necks someday," she could hear her mother saying. "It's pretty, though." The Indian weaving of the hawk at sunrise, all black and red, hung on the far left wall.

She thought of her mother, a small, quick woman with bronze, close-curling hair cut short, eager to have what she thought of as "just the right thing," wandering distant markets, seeking out things for the cottage. It seemed to Rosalind that when she opened the door past the stairwell into the bedroom that her parents had used, that surely she would find that choosing, active ghost in motion over a chest or moving a curtain at the window, and that surely, ascending the dangerous stair to look into the two bedrooms above, she would hear the quick voice say, "Oh, it's you, Rosalind, now you just tell me . . ." But everything was silent.

Rosalind came downstairs. She returned to the front door and saw that Mr. Thibodeau had driven away. Had he said something about going back for something? She closed the door quietly, reentered the big natural room, and let the things there speak.

For it was all self-contained, knowing and infinitely quiet. The lake gave its perpetual lapping sound, like nibbling fish in shallow water, now and then splashing up, as though a big one had flourished. Lap, lap against the wooden piles that supported the balcony. Lap against the steps, with a swishing motion on the lowest one, a passing-over instead of an against sound. The first steps were replaced, new, the color fresh blond instead of worn brown. The room heard the lapping, the occasional splash, the swish of water.

Rosalind herself was being got through to by something even less predictable than water. What she heard was memory: voices quarreling. From three years ago they woke to life. A slant of light—that had brought them back. Just at this time of day, she had been coming in from swimming. The voices had climbed the large, clear windows, clawing for exit, and finding none, had fled like people getting out of a burning theater, through the door to the far right that opened out onto the balcony. She had been coming up the steps from the water when the voices stampeded over her, frightening, intense, racing outward from the panic within. "You know you do and you know you will . . . there's no use to lie, I've been through all that. Helpless is all I can feel, all I can be. That's the awful part . . . !" "I didn't drive all this way just to get back into that. Go on, get away to New York with dear Aunt Mildred. Who's to know, for that matter, if it's Mildred at all?" "You hide your life like a card in the deck and then have the nerve—! Oh, you're a great magician, aren't you?" "Hush, she's out there . . . hush, now . . . you must realize—" "I do nothing but realize—" "Hush . . . just . . . no . . ." And their known selves returned to them as she came in, dripping, pretending nothing had happened, gradually believing her own pretense.

The way she'd learned to do, all the other times. Sitting forgotten, for the moment, in an armchair too big back in New York, listening while her heart hurt until her mother said, "Darling, go to your room, I'll be there in a minute." Even on vacation, it was sometimes the same thing. And Mother coming in later, as she half slept, half waited, to hold her hand and say, "Just forget it now, tomorrow it won't seem real. We all love each other. Tomorrow you won't even remember." Kissed and tucked in, she trusted. It didn't happen all the time. And the tomorrows were clear and bright. The only trouble was, this time there hadn't been any tomorrow, only the tomorrow of her mother's driving away. Could anybody who sounded like that, saying those things, have a wreck the very next morning and those things have nothing to do with it?

Maybe I got the times mixed up.

("She had just a little part in the cast of the show he worked with last year." "That's how they met, was it?") ("Your mother got the vapors sometimes. The theater scared her." She'd heard her father say that.)

I dreamed it all, she thought, and couldn't be sure this wasn't true, though wondered if she could dream so vividly that she could see the exact print of her wet foot just through the doorway there, beside it the drying splash from the water's runnel down her leg. But it could have been another day.

Why not just ask Daddy?

At the arrival of this simple solution, she let out a long sigh, flung her hands back of her head, and stretched out on the beautiful rug her mother had placed there. Her eyes dimmed; she felt the lashes flutter downward. . . .

A footstep and a voice awakened her from how short a sleep she did not know. Rolling over and sitting up, she saw a strange woman—short, heavyset, with faded skin, gray hair chopped off around her face, plain run-down shoes. She was wearing slacks. Then she smiled and things about her changed.

"You don't remember me, do you? I'm Marie Thibodeau. I remember you and your mom and your dad. That was all bad. *Gros dommage.* But you're back now. You'll have a good time again, eh? We thought maybe you didn't have nothing you could eat yet. You come back with me. I going make you some nice lunch. My husband said to come find you."

She rose slowly, walked through shadows toward the woman, who still had something of the quality of an apparition. Did she think that because of her mother, others must have died too? She followed. The lunch was the same as years before: the meat pie, the beans, the catsup and relish and the white bread taken sliced from its paper. And the talk, too, was nearly the same: kind things said before, repeated now; chewed, swallowed.

"You don't remember me, but I remember you. You're *the* Nat Jennings's daughter, used to come here with your folks." This was what the boy said, in Howard Johnson's.

"We're the tennis ones—Dunbar," said the girl, who was his sister, not his date; for saying "tennis" had made Rosalind remember the big house their family owned— "the villa," her father called it—important grounds around it, and a long frontage on the lake. She remembered them as strutting around, smaller then, holding rackets that looked too large for their bodies. They had been allowed on the court only at certain hours, along with their friends, but even then they had wished to be observed. Now here they were before her, grown up and into denim, like anybody else. Paul and Elaine. They had showed up at the entrance to the motel restaurant, tan and healthy. Paul had acquired a big smile; Elaine a breathless, hesitating voice, the kind Daddy didn't like, it was so intended to tease.

"Let's all find a booth together," Paul Dunbar said.

Rosalind said, "I spent half the afternoon with the telephone man, the other half at the grocery. Getting the cottage opened."

"You can come up to our house after we eat. Not much open here yet. We're on spring holidays."

"They extended it. Outbreak of measles."

"She made that up," said the Dunbar boy, who was speaking straight and honestly to Rosalind. "We told them we had got sick and would be back next week."

"It's because we are so in-tell-i-gent. . . . Making our grades is not a prob-lem," Elaine said in her trick voice.

"We've got the whole house to ourselves. Our folks won't be coming till June. Hey, why don't you move down with us?"

"I can't," said Rosalind. "Daddy's coming up tomorrow. And my stepmother. He got married again."

"Your parents split?"

"No . . . I mean, not how you think. My mother was killed three years ago, driving in New York. She had a wreck."

"Jesus, what a break. I'm sorry, Rosalind."

"You heard about it, Paul. We both did."

"It's still a tough break."

"Mr. Thibodeau's been helping me. Mrs. Thibodeau's cleaning up. They're coming tomorrow." If this day is ever over.

She went with them after dinner. . . .

The Dunbar house could be seen from the road, a large two-story house on the lake, with white wood trim. There were two one-story wings, like smaller copies of the central house, their entrances opening at either side, the right one on a flagstone walk, winding through a sloping lawn, the left on a porte-cochere, where the Dunbars parked. Within, the large rooms were shuttered, the furniture dust-covered. The three of them went to the glassed-in room on the opposite wing and put some records on. They danced on the tiled floor amid the white wicker furniture.

Had they heard a knocking or hadn't they? A strange boy was standing in the doorway, materialized. Elaine had cried, "Oh goodness, Fenwick, you scared me!" She moved back from Paul's controlling rhythm. They were all facing the stranger. He was heavier than Paul; he was tall and grown to the measure of his big hands and feet. He looked serious and easily detachable from the surroundings; it wasn't possible to guess by looking at him where he lived or what he was doing there.

"Fenwick . . ." Paul was saying to him. What sort of name was that? He strode over to the largest chaise longue, and fitted himself into it. Paul introduced Rosalind to Fenwick.

"I have a mile-long problem to solve before Thursday," Fenwick said. "I'm getting cross-eyed. You got a beer?"

"Fenwick is a math-uh-mat-i-cul gene-i-yus," Elaine told Rosalind. The record finished and she switched off the machine.

"Fenwick wishes he was," said Fenwick.

It seemed that they were all at some school together, called

Wakeley, over in Vermont. They knew people to talk about together. "I've been up about umpteen hours," Rosalind said. "I came all the way from New York this morning."

"Just let me finish this beer, and I'll take you home," said Fenwick.

"It's just Howard Johnson's," she said.

"There are those that call it home," said Fenwick, downing beer.

They walked together to the highway, where Fenwick had left his little old rickety car. The trees were bursting from the bud, you could practically smell them grow, but the branches were still dark, and cold-looking and wet, because it had rained while they were inside. The damp road seamed beneath the tires. There were not many people around. She hugged herself into her raincoat.

"The minute I saw you I remembered you," Fenwick said. "I just felt like we were friends. You used to go to that little park with all the other kids. Your daddy would put you on the seesaw. He pushed it up and down for you. But I don't guess you'd remember me."

"I guess I ought to," Rosalind said. "Maybe you grew a lot."

"You can sure say that. They thought I wasn't going to stop." The sign ahead said "Howard Johnson's." "I'd do my problem better if we had some coffee."

"Tomorrow maybe," she said. "I'm dead tired." But what she thought was, He likes me.

At the desk she found three messages, all from Daddy and Eva. "Call when you come in." "Call as soon as you can." "Call even if late." She called.

"So it'll be late tomorrow, maybe around dinner. What happened was . . ." He went on and on. With Nat Jennings, you got used to postponements, so her mother always said. "How's it going, Rosie? I've thought about you every minute."

"Everything's ready for you, or it will be when you come."

"Don't cook up a special dinner. We might be late. It's a long road."

In a dream her mother was walking with her. They were in the library at Lake George. In the past her mother had often gone there to check out books. She was waiting for a certain book she wanted, but it hadn't come back yet. "But you did promise me last week," she was saying to somebody at the desk; then she was walking up the street with Rosalind, and Rosalind saw the book in her shopping bag. "You got it after all," she said to her mother. "I just found it lying there on the walk," her mother said, and then Rosalind remembered how she had leaned down to pick up something. "That's nice," said Rosalind, satisfied that things could happen this way. "I think it's nice, too," said her mother, and they went along together.

By noon the next day her work was done, but she felt bad because she had found something—a scarf in one of the dresser drawers. It was a sumptuous French satin scarf in a jagged play of colors, mainly red, a shade her mother, with her coppery hair, had never worn. It smelled of Eva's perfume. So they had been up here before, she thought, but why—this far from New York? And why not say so? Helpless was what her mother said she felt. Can I, thought Rosalind, ask Daddy about this, too?

In the afternoon she drove up into the Adirondacks with Elaine and Paul Dunbar. They took back roads, a minor highway that crossed from the lakeshore road to the Thruway; another beyond that threaded along the bulging sides of the mountains. They passed one lake after another: some small and limpid; others half-choked with water lilies and thickly shaded where frogs by the hundreds were chorusing, invisible amid the fresh lime-green; and some larger still, marked with stumps of trees mysteriously broken off. From one of these, strange birdcalls sounded. Then the road ran upward. Paul pulled up under some tall pines and stopped.

"We're going to climb," he announced.

It suited Rosalind because Elaine had just asked her to tell her "all about the theater, every single thing you know." She wouldn't have to do that, at least. Free of the car, they stood still in deserted air. There was no feel of houses near. The brother and sister started along a path they apparently knew. It led higher, winding through trees, with occasional glimpses of a rotting lake below and promise of some triumphant view above. Rosalind followed next to Paul, with Elaine trailing behind. Under a big oak they stopped to rest.

Through the leaves a small view opened up; there was a little valley below, with a stream running through it. The three of them sat hugging their knees and talking, once their breath came back. "Very big deal," Paul was saying. "Five people sent home, weeping parents outside offices, and everybody tiptoeing past. About what? The whole school smokes pot, everybody knows it. Half the profs were on it. Remember old Borden?"

Elaine's high-pitched laugh. "He said, 'Just going for a joint,' when he pushed into the john one day. Talking back over his shoulder."

"What really rocked the boat was when everybody started cheating. Plain and fancy."

"What made them start?" Rosalind asked. Pot was passed around at her school, too, in the Upper Eighties, but you could get into trouble about it.

"You know Miss Hollander was heard to say out loud one day, 'The dean's a shit.' "

"That's the source of the whole fucking mess," said Paul. "The stoopid dean's a shit."

"Is he a fag?" asked Rosalind, not too sure of language like this.

"Not even that," said Paul, and picked up a rock to throw.

He put down his hand to Rosalind. "Come on, we got a little farther to climb."

The path snaked sharply upward. She followed his long legs and brown loafers, one with the stitching breaking at the top, and stopping for breath, she looked back and discovered they were alone. "Where's Elaine?"

"She's lazy." He stopped high above to wait for her. She looked up to him and saw him turn to face her, jeans tight over his narrow thighs and flat waist. He put a large hand down to pull her up, and grinned as she came unexpectedly too fast; being thin and light, she sailed up so close they bumped together. His face skin was glossy with sweat. "Just a little farther," he encouraged her. His front teeth were not quite even. Light exploded from the tips of his ears. Grappling at roots, avoiding sheer surfaces of rock, gaining footholds on patches of earth, they burst finally out on a ledge of rough but fairly flat stone, chiseled away as though in a quarry, overlooking a dizzying sweep of New York countryside. "Oh." Rosalind caught her breath. "How gorgeous! We live high up with a terrace over Central Park," she confided excitedly. "But that's nothing like this!"

Paul put his arm around her. "Don't get too close. You know some people just love heights. They love 'em to death. Just show them one and off they go."

"Not me."

"Come here." He led her a little to the side, placing her—"Not there, here"—at a spot where two carved lines crossed, as though Indians had marked it for something. Then, his arm close around her, he pressed his mouth down on hers. Her long brown hair fell backward over his shoulder. If she struggled, she might pull them both over the edge. "Don't." She broke her mouth away. His free hand was kneading her.

"Why? Why not?" The words burrowed into her ear like objects.

"I hadn't thought of you . . . not for myself."

"Think of me now. Let's just stay here a minute."

But she slipped away and went sliding back down. Arriving in the level space with a torn jacket and a skinned elbow, she found Elaine lying back against a rock, apparently sleeping. A camera with a telescope lens was resting on the canvas shoulder bag she had carried up the hill.

Elaine sat up, opening her eyes. Rosalind stopped, and Paul's heavy stride, overtaking, halted close behind her. She did not want to look at him, and was rubbing at the blood speckled out on her scratched arm where she'd fallen against a limb.

"Paul thinks he's ir-ree-sisty-bul," Elaine said. "Now we know it isn't so."

Looking up, Rosalind could see the lofty ledge where she and Paul had been. Elaine picked up the camera, detached the lens, and fitted both into the canvas bag. "Once I took a whole home movie. That was the time he was screwing the waitress from the pizza place."

"Oh, sure, get funny," said Paul. He had turned an angry red.

In the car, Elaine leaned back to speak to Rosalind. "We're known to be a little bit crazy. Don't you worry, Ros-uh-lind."

Paul said nothing. He drove hunched forward over the wheel.

"Last summer was strictly crazy, start to finish," said Elaine. "Wasn't that true, Paul?"

"It was pretty crazy," said Paul. "Rosalind would have loved it," he added. He was getting mad at her now, she thought.

She asked to hop out at the road to the cottage, instead of going to the motel. She said she wanted to see Mr. Thibodeau.

"Sorry you didn't like the view," said Paul from the wheel. He was laughing now; his mood had changed.

Once they'd vanished, she walked down the main road to the Fenwick mailbox.

. . .

From the moment she left the road behind she had to climb again, not as strenuously as up to the mountain ledge, but a slow, winding climb up an ill-tended road. The house that finally broke into view after a sharp turn was bare of paint and run-down. There was a junk car in the wide yard, the parts just about picked off it, one side sitting on planks, and a litter of household odds and ends nearby. A front porch, sagging, was covered with a tangle of what looked to be hunting and camping things. From behind, a dog barked, a warning sound to let her know who was in charge. There was mud in the path to the door.

Through the window of a tacked-on wing to the right, there was Fenwick, sure enough, at a table with peeling paint, in a plain kitchen chair, bending over a large notebook. Textbooks and graph papers were scattered around him. She rapped on the pane and summoned his attention, as though from another planet. He came to the door.

"Oh, it's you, Rose."

"Rosalind."

"I'm working on my problem." He came out and joined her. Maybe he was a genius, Rosalind thought, to have got a fellowship to that school, making better grades than the Dunbars.

"I've been out with Paul and Elaine."

"Don't tell me Paul took you up to that lookout."

She nodded. They sat down on a bench that seemed about to fall in.

"Dunbar's got a collection of pictures—girls he's got to go up there. It's just a dumb gimmick."

"He thinks it's funny," she said, and added, "I left."

"Good. They're on probation, you know. All that about school's being suspended's not true. I'm out for another reason, studying for honors. But—"

A window ran up. A woman's voice came around the side of the house. "Henry, I told you—"

"But I need a break, Mother," he said, without turning his head.

"Is your name Henry?" Rosalind asked.

"So they tell me. Come on, I'll take you back where you're staying."

"I just wanted to see where you lived." He didn't answer. Probably it wasn't the right thing. He walked her down the hill, talking all the way, and put her into his old Volkswagen.

"The Dunbars stick too close together. You'd think they weren't kin. They're like a couple dating. They make up these jokes on people. I was there the other night to help them through some math they failed. But it didn't turn out that way. Know why? They've got no mind for work. They think something will happen, so they won't have to." He hesitated, silent, as the little car swung in and out of the wooded curves. "I think they make love," he said, very low. It was a kind of gossip. "There's talk at school. . . . Now don't go and tell about it."

"You're warning me," she said.

"That's it. There's people living back in the woods, no different from them. Mr. Thibodeau and Papa—they hunt bear together, way off from here, high up. Last winter I went, too, and there was a blizzard. We shot a bear but it looked too deep a snow to get the carcass out, but we did, after a day or so. We stayed with these folks, brother and sister. Some odd little kids running around.

"If they get thrown out of Wakeley, they can go somewhere else. Their folks have a lot of money. So no problem."

"But I guess anywhere you have to study," said Rosalind.

He had brought her to the motel, and now they got out and walked to a plot where shrubs were budding on the slant of hill above the road. Fenwick had speculative eyes that kept to themselves, and a frown from worry or too many figures, just a small thread between his light eyebrows.

"When I finish my problem, any minute now, I'll go back to school."

"My mother died three years ago, in June," said Rosalind.

"I knew that. It's too bad, Rosalind. I'm sorry."

"Did you know her?" Rosalind experienced an eagerness, expectation, as if she doubted her mother's ever having been known.

"I used to see her with you," said Fenwick. "So I guess I'd know her if I saw her." His hand had appeared on her shoulder. She was at about the right height for that.

"Nobody will ever see her again," she said. He pulled her closer.

"If I come back in the summer, I'd like to see you, Rosalind."

"Me, too," she said.

"I've got some stuff you can read." He was squinting. The sun had come through some pale clouds.

"Things you wrote?" She wondered at him.

"I do a lot of things. I'll have a car." He glanced toward it doubtfully. "It's not much of a car, though."

"It's a fine car," she said, so he could walk off to it, feeling all right, and wave to her.

Rosalind was surprised and obscurely hurt by the message she received at the motel: namely, that her father and stepmother had already arrived and had called by for her. She had some money left over from what her father had given her, and not wanting to call, she took a taxi down to the cottage.

Her hurt sprang from thwarted plans. She had meant to prepare for them, greet them, have dinner half done, develop a festive air. Now they would be greeting her.

In the taxi past Mr. Thibodeau's house, she saw a strange car coming toward them that made them draw far to one side, sink treacherously among loose fallen leaves. A Chevrolet sedan went past; the man within, a stranger, was well dressed and wore a hat. He looked up to nod at the driver and glance keenly within at his passenger.

"Who was that?" Rosalind asked.

"Griffin, I think his name is," the driver said. "Real estate," he added.

There had been a card stuck in the door when she had come, Rosalind recalled, and a printed message: "Thinking of selling? Griffin's the Guy."

Then she was alighting, crying, "Daddy! Eva! It's me!" And they were running out, crying, "There she is! You got the call?" Daddy was tossing her, forgetting she'd grown; he almost banged her head against a beam. "You nearly knocked my three brains out," she laughed. "It's beautiful!" Eva cried, about the cottage. She spread her arms wide as wings and swirled across the rugs in a solo dance. "It's simply charming!"

Daddy opened the piano with a flourish. He began thumping the old keys, some of which had gone dead from the damp. But "Sweet Rosie O'Grady" was unmistakably coming out. They were hugging and making drinks and going out to look at the boat, kneeling down to test the still stone-chill water.

"What good taste your mother had!" Eva told her, smiling. "The apartment . . . now this!" She was kind.

In the late afternoon Rosalind and her father lowered and launched the canoe, and finding that it floated without a leak and sat well in the water, they decided to test it. Daddy had changed his gray slacks and blazer for gabardine trousers and a leather jacket. He wore a denim shirt. Daddy glistened with life, and what he wore was more important than what other people wore. He thought of clothes, evidently, but he never, that she could remember, discussed them. They simply appeared on him, like various furs or fleece that he could shed suddenly and grow just as suddenly new. Above button-down collars or open-throated knit pullovers or turtlenecks or black bow ties, his face, with its slightly ruddy look, even in winter, its cleft chin and radiating crinkles, was like a law of attraction, drawing whatever interested, whatever lived. In worry or grief, he hid it, that face. Then the clothes no longer mattered. Rosalind had sometimes found him in a room alone near a window, still, his face bent down behind one shoulder covered with some old faded shirt, only the top of his head showing and that revealed as startlingly gray, the hair growing thin. But when the face came up, it would seem to resume its livingness as naturally as breath, his hair being the same as ever, barely sprinkled with gray. It was the face for her, his gift.

"Did you see the real estate man?" Rosalind asked over her shoulder, paddling with an out-of-practice wobble.

"Griffin? Oh, yes, he was here. Right on the job, those guys."

They paddled along, a stone's throw from the shore. To their right the lake stretched out wide and sunlit. One or two distant fishing boats dawdled near a small island. The lake, a creamy blue, flashed now and again in air that was still sharp.

"Daddy, did you know Eva a long time?"

There was a silence from behind her. "Not too long." Then he said what he'd said before. "She was a member of the cast. Rosie, we shouldn't have let you go off by yourself. I realized that this morning. I woke up early thinking it, and jumped straight out of bed. By six I'd packed. Who've you been seeing?"

"I ran into the Dunbars, Paul and Elaine, down in the big white house, you know. They're here from school. I have to run from Mrs. Thibodeau. She wants to catch and feed me. And then there's Fenwick."

"Some old guy up the hill who sells junk . . . is that the one?"

"No, his son. He's a mathematical genius, Daddy."

"Beware of mathematical geniuses," her father said, "especially if their fathers sell junk."

"You always told me that," said Rosalind. "I just forgot."

When they came in they were laughing. She and Eva cooked the meals. Daddy played old records, forgoing gin rummy for once. That was the first day.

"Wait! Look now! Look!"

It was Eva speaking while Daddy blindfolded Rosalind. They had built a fire. Somebody had found in a shop uptown the sort of stuff you threw on it to make it sparkle. The room on a gloomy afternoon, though shut up tight against a heavy drizzle, was full of warmth and light. Elaine and Paul Dunbar were there, sitting on the couch. Fenwick was there, choosing to crouch down on a hassock in the corner like an Indian, no matter how many times he was offered a chair. He had been followed in by one of the Fenwick dogs, a huge German shepherd with a bushy, perfectly curling tail lined with white, which he waved at times from side to side like a plume, and when seated, furled about his paws. He smelled like a wet dog owned by a junk dealer.

At the shout of "Look now!" Daddy whipped off the blindfold. The cake had been lighted—eighteen candles—a shining delight. They had cheated a little to have a party for Rosalind; her birthday wasn't till the next week. But the idea was fun. Eva had thought of it because she had found a box full of party things in the unused bedroom: tinsel, sparklers, masks, and a crepe-paper tablecloth with napkins. She had poured rum into some cherry Kool-Aid and floated orange slices across the top. She wore a printed off-the-shoulder blouse with a denim skirt and espadrilles. Her big glasses glanced back fire and candlelight. The young people watched her lighting candles for the table with a long, fancy match held in brightly tipped fingers. Daddy took the blue bandanna blindfold and wound it pirate-fashion around his forehead. He had contrived an eye patch for one eye. "Back in the fifties these things were a status symbol," he said, "but I forget what status they symbolized."

"Two-car garage but no Cadillac," Paul said.

Daddy winked at Elaine. "My daughter's friends get prettier every day."

"So does your daughter," Paul said.

Eva passed them paper plates of birthday cake.

"*She's* getting to the dangerous age, not me. Hell, I was there all the time."

Everyone laughed but Fenwick. He fed small bites of cake to the dog and large ones to himself, while Rosalind refilled his glass.

The friends had brought her presents. A teddy bear dressed in blue jeans from Elaine. A gift-shop canoe in birchbark from Paul. The figure of an old man carved in wood from Fenwick. His father had done it, he said. Rosalind held it up. She set it down. He watched her. He was redeeming his father, whom nobody thought much of. "It's grand," she said, "I love it." Fenwick sat with his hand buried in the dog's thick ruff. His nails, cleaned up for coming there, would get grimy in the dog's coat.

Rosalind's father so far had ignored Fenwick. He was sitting on a stool near Elaine and Paul, talking about theater on campuses, how most campus musicals went dead on Broadway, the rare one might survive, but usually . . . Eva approached the dog, who growled at her. "He won't bite," said Fenwick.

"Is a mathematician liable to know whether or not a dog will bite?" Eva asked.

"Why not?" asked Fenwick.

"You've got quite a reputation to live up to," Eva pursued.

She was kneeling near him, close enough to touch, holding her gaze, like her voice, very steady. "I hear you called a genius more often than not."

"You can have a genius rating in something without setting the world on fire," said Fenwick. "A lot of people who've got them are just walking around doing dumb things, the same as anybody."

"I'll have to think that over," Eva said.

There came a heavy pounding at the door, and before anybody could go to it, a man with a grizzled beard, weathered skin, battered clothes, and a rambling walk entered the room. He looked all around until he found Fenwick. "There you are," he said.

Rosalind's father had risen. Nobody said anything. "I'm Nat Jennings." Daddy put out his hand. "This is my wife. What can we do for you?"

"It's my boy," said Fenwick's father, shaking hands. "His mother was looking for him, something she's wanting him for. I thought if he wasn't doing nothing . . ."

"Have a drink," said Nat.

"Just pour it straight out of the bottle," said Fenwick's father, who had taken the measure of the punch.

Fenwick got up. "That's O.K., Mr. Jennings. I'll just go on with Papa."

The dog had moved to acknowledge Mr. Fenwick, who had downed his drink already. Now the boy came to them both, the dog being no longer his. He turned to the rest of the room, which seemed suddenly to be of a different race. "We'll go," he said. He turned again at the living-room entrance. "Thanks."

Rosalind ran after them. She stood in the front door, hidden by the wall of the entrance from those in the room, and leaned out into the rain. "Oh, Mr. Fenwick, I love the carving you did!"

He glanced back. "Off on a bear hunt, deep in the snow. Had to do something."

"Goodbye, Fenwick. Thanks for coming!"

He stopped to answer, but said nothing. For a moment his look was like a voice, crying out to her from across something. For the first time in her life, Rosalind felt the force that pulls stronger than any other. Just to go with him, to be, even invisibly, near. Then the three of them—tall boy, man, and dog, stair-stepped together—were walking away on the rainy path.

When she went inside, she heard Paul Dunbar recalling how Nat Jennings used to organize a fishing derby back in one of the little lakes each summer. He would get the lake stocked, and everybody turned out with casting rods and poles to fish it out. (Rosalind remembered; she had ridden on his shoulder everywhere, till suddenly, one summer, she had got too big for that, and once it had rained.) "And then there were those funny races down in the park—you folks put them on. One year I won a prize!" (Oh, that too, she remembered, her mother running with two giant orange bows like chrysanthemums, held in either hand, orange streamers flying, her coppery hair in the sun.) "You ought to get all that started again."

"It sounds grand, but I guess you'd better learn how yourselves," Eva was saying. "We'll probably not be up here at all."

"Not be here!" Rosalind's cry as she returned from the door was like an alarm. "Not be here!" A silence was suddenly on them.

Her father glanced up, but straightened out smoothly. "Of course we'll be here. We'll have to work on it together."

It had started raining harder. Paul and Elaine, though implored to stay, left soon.

When the rain chilled the air, Eva had got out a fringed Spanish shawl, embroidered in bright flowers on a metallic gold background. Her glasses above this, plus one of the silly hats she'd found, made her seem a many-tiered fantasy of a woman, concocted by Picasso, or made to be carried through the streets for some Latin holiday parade.

Light of movement, wearing a knit tie, cuff links on his striped shirt ("In your honor," he said to Rosalind), impeccable blue blazer above gray slacks, Nat Jennings played the country gentleman with pleasure to himself and everyone. His pretty daughter at her birthday party was his delight. This was what his every move had been saying. And now she had gone to her room. He was knocking on its door. "Rosie?"

"I'm drunk," said Rosalind.

He laughed. "We're going to talk at dinner, Rosie. When you sober up, come down. Did you enjoy your birthday party, baby?"

"Sure I did."

"I like your friends."

"Thank you."

"Too bad about Fenwick's father. That boy deserves better."

"I guess so."

She was holding an envelope Paul had slipped into her hand when he left. It had a photo and its negative enclosed, the one on the high point, the two of them kissing. The note said, "We're leaving tomorrow, sorry if I acted stupid. When we come back, maybe we can try some real ones. Paul."

There won't be any coming back for me, she lay thinking, dazed. But this was your place, Mother. Mother, what do I do now?

He was waiting for her at the bottom of the stairs and treated her with delightful solemnity, as though she were the visiting daughter of an old friend. He showed her to her place and held the chair for her. Eva, now changed into slacks, a silk shirt, and nubby sweater, came in with a steaming casserole. The candles were lighted again.

"I'm not a grand cook, as Rose knows." She smiled. "But you couldn't be allowed, on your birthday . . ."

"She's read a hole in the best cookbook," said Daddy.

"I'm sure it's great," Rosalind said in a little voice, and felt tension pass from one of them to the other.

"I'm in love with Fenwick," Eva announced, and dished out coq au vin.

"Won't get you anywhere," Daddy said. "I see the whole thing: he's gone on Rosie, but she's playing it cool."

"They're all going back tomorrow," Rosalind said. "Elaine and Paul were just on suspension, and Fenwick's finished his problem."

They were silent, passing dishes. Daddy and Eva exchanged glances.

"Rosie," said Daddy, filling everyone's wineglass, "we've been saving our good news till after your party. Now we want you to know. You remember the little off-Broadway musical I worked with last fall? Well, Hollywood is picking it up at quite a hefty sum. It's been in negotiation for two months. Now all's clear, and they're wanting to hire me along with the purchase. Best break I ever had."

"I'm so happy I could walk on air," said Eva.

"Are we going to *move* there!" Rosalind felt numb.

"Of course not, baby. There'll be trips, some periods out there, nothing permanent."

Before Rosalind suddenly, as she glanced from one of them to the other, they grew glossy in an extra charge of flesh and beauty. A log even broke in the fireplace, and a flame reached to some of the sparkler powder that was unignited, so that it flared up as though to hail them. They grew great as faces on a drive-in movie screen, seen floating up out of nowhere along a highway; they might mount skyward any minute and turn to constellations. He had wanted something big to happen, she knew, for a long time. "They never give me any credit" was a phrase she knew by heart. Staying her own human size, Rosalind knew that all they were saying was probably true. They had shoved her birthday up by a week to tidy her away, but they didn't look at it that way, she had to guess.

"Let's drink a toast to Daddy!" she cried, and drained her wineglass.

"Rosalind!" her father scolded happily. "What does anyone do with an alcoholic child?"

"Straight to AA," Eva filled in, "the minute we return."

"Maybe there's a branch in Lake George," Daddy worried.

"I'll cause spectacles at the Plaza," Rosalind giggled through the dizziness of wine. "I'll dance on the bar and jump in the fountain. You'll be so famous it'll make the *Daily News*."

"I've even got some dessert," said Eva, who, now the news was out, had the air of someone who intends to wait on people as seldom as possible. The cottage looked plainer and humbler all the time. How could they stand it for a single other night? Rosalind wondered. They would probably just explode out of there by some chemical process of rejection that not even Fenwick could explain.

"If things work out," Daddy was saying, "we may get to make Palm Beach winters yet. No use to plan ahead."

"Would you like that?" Rosalind asked Eva, as if she didn't know.

"Why, I just tag along with the family," Eva said. "Your rules are mine."

That night Rosalind slipped out of her upstairs room. In order to avoid the Thibodeaus, whose house had eyes and ears, she skirted through the woods and ran into part of the lake, which appeared unexpectedly before her, like a person. She bogged in spongy loam and slipped on mossy rocks, and shivered, drenched to the knees, in the chill night shade of early foliage. At last she came out of shadow onto a road, but not before some large shape, high up, had startled her, blundering among the branches. A car went past and in the glancing headlights she saw the mailbox and its lettering and turned to climb the steep road up to the Fenwicks'. What did she expect to happen there? Just whom did she expect to find? Fenwick himself, of course, but in what way? To lead her out of here, take her somewhere, take her off for good? Say she could stay on with him, and they'd get the cottage someday and share it forever? That would be her dream, even if Fenwick's daddy camped on them and smelled up the place with whiskey.

She climbed with a sense of the enveloping stillness of the woods, the breath of the lake, the distant appeal of the mountains. The road made its final turn to the right, just before the yard. But at that point she was surprised to hear, as if growing out of the wood itself, murmurous voices, not one or two, but apparently by the dozen, and the sound of a throbbing guitar string, interposing from one pause to the next. She inched a little closer and stopped in the last of the black shade. A fire was burning in a wire grating near the steps. Tatters of flame leaped up, making the shadows blacker. High overhead, the moon shone. Fenwick, too, was entitled to a last night at home, having finished some work nobody else could have understood. He would return that summer. He was sitting on the edge of the porch, near a post. Some others were on the steps, or on chairs outside, or even on the ground.

They were humming some tune she didn't know and she heard a voice rise, Mrs. Thibodeau's beyond a doubt! "Now I never said I knew that from a firsthand look, but I'd have to suppose as much." Then Mr. Thibodeau was joining in: "Seen her myself . . . more than a time or two." The Thibodeaus were everywhere, with opinions to express, but about what and whom? All went foundering in an indistinct mumble of phrases until a laugh rose and then another stroke across the strings asked them to sing together, a song she'd never heard. "Now that's enough," a woman's voice said. "I ain't pitching no more tunes." "I've sung all night, many's the time." "Just you and your jug."

From near the steps a shape rose suddenly; it was one of the dogs, barking on the instant of rising—there had been a shift of wind. He trotted toward her. She stood still. Now the snuffling muzzle ranged over her. The great tail moved its slow white fan. It was the one she knew. She patted the intelligent head. Someone whistled. It was Fenwick, who, she could see, had risen from his seat.

Something fell past him, out of the thick-bunched human shapes on the porch. It had been pushed or shoved and was yelling, a child. "Stealing cake again," some voice said, and the body hit the ground with a thump. The mother in the chair, not so much as turning, said, "Going to break ever' bone in her one o' these days." "Serve her right" came from the background—Mr. Fenwick. It was young Fenwick himself who finally went down to pick her up (by the back of her shirt, like a puppy), Mrs. Thibodeau who came to dust her off. The yelling stopped. "Hush now," said Mrs. Thibodeau. Rosalind turned and went away.

"Who's there?" Fenwick was calling toward the road. "Nobody," a man's voice, older, said. "Wants his girlfriend," said the father. "Go and git her, fella."

The mountain went on talking. Words faded to murmurs, losing outline; as she stumbled down turns of road, they lost even echoes. She was alone where she had not meant to be, but for all that, strangely detached, elated.

Back on the paved road, she padded along in sneakers. Moonlight lay bright in patterns through the trees. Finally the Dunbar house rose up, moonlight brightening one white portico, while the other stood almost eclipsed in darkness. In a lighted interior, through a downstairs window, she could see them, one standing, the other looking up, graceful hands making gestures, mouths moving—together and alone. Great white moths circling one another, planning, loving maybe.

She thought they were like the photographs they took. The negative is me, she thought.

Far up the road, so far it tired her almost as much to think of it as to walk it, the old resort hotel looked out on Lake George with hundreds of empty windows, eyes with vision gone, the porticoes reaching wide their outspread arms. Water lapped with none to hear. "No Trespassing," said the sign, and other signs said "For Sale," like children calling to one another.

Rosalind looked up. Between her and the road, across the lawn, a brown bear was just standing up. He was turning his head this way and that. The head was small, wedge-shaped. The bear's pelt moved when he did, like grass in a breeze. Pointing her way, the head stopped still. She felt the gaze thrill through her with long foreverness, then drop away. On all fours, he looked small, and moved toward the lake with feet shuffling close together, rather like a rolling ball, loose and tumbling toward the water. The moon sent a shimmering golden path across the lake. She was just remembering that her mother, up here alone with her, claimed to have seen a bear late at night, looking through the window. Daddy didn't doubt she'd dreamed it. He didn't think they came so close. Rosalind knew herself as twice seen and twice known now, by dog and bear. She walked the road home.

Voices sounding in her head, Rosalind twisted and turned that night, sleepless. She got up once, and taking the red scarf she had found from the drawer, she put it down on the living-room table near the large vase of money plant. Then she went back up and slept, what night was left of it.

Daddy came in for Eva's coffee and then they both appeared, he freshly shaved and she perfect in her smooth makeup, a smartly striped caftan flowing to her ankles. Rosalind had crept down in wrinkled pajamas, her bare feet warping back from the chill floor.

"Today's for leaving," her father said. When Rosalind dropped her gaze, he observed her. They were standing in the kitchen before the stove. They were alone. He was neat, fit, in slacks, a beige shirt checked in brown and blue, and a foulard—affected for anyone but him. His amber eyes fixed on her blue ones, offered pools of sincerity for her to plunge into.

"What's this?" Eva asked. She came in with the scarf.

"I found it," said Rosalind. "Isn't it yours?"

Eva looked over her head at Nat. "It must have been your mother's."

"No," said Rosalind. "It wasn't."

After breakfast, by common consent, Rosalind and her father rose from the table and went down to the boat. Together they paddled out to the island. They had done this often in the past. The island was inviting, slanted like a turtle's back, rich with clumps of birch and bushes, trimmed with gray rock. Out there today, their words emerged suddenly, like thoughts being printed on the air.

"We aren't coming back," said Rosalind. "This is all."

"I saw you come in last night."

A bird flew up out of the trees.

"Did you tell Eva?"

"She was asleep. Why?"

"She'll think I just sneaked off to see Fenwick. But I didn't. I went off myself . . . by myself."

He played with rocks, seated, forearms resting on his knees, looking at the lake. "I won't tell."

"I wanted to find Mother."

"Did you?"

"In a way . . . I know she's here, all around here. Don't you?"

"I think she might be most everywhere."

Maybe what he was saying was something about himself. The ground was being shifted; they were debating without saying so, and he was changing things around without saying so.

"I let you come up here alone," he went on, "because I thought you needed it—your time alone. Maybe I was wrong."

"If you'd just say you see it too."

"See what?"

"What I was saying. That she's here. No other places. Here."

The way he didn't answer her was so much a silence she could hear the leaves stir. "You didn't love her." The words fell from her, by themselves, you'd have to think, because she hadn't willed them to. They came out because they were there.

"Fool! Of course I did!"

Long after, she realized he had shouted, screamed almost. She didn't know it at the moment, because her eyes had blurred with what she'd accused him of, and her hearing, too, had gone with her sight. She was barely clinging to the world.

When her vision cleared, she looked for him and saw that he was lying down on gray rock with his eyes closed, facing upward, exactly as though exhausted from a task. Like the reverse picture on a face card, he looked to be duplicating an opposite image of his straight-up self; only the marked cleft in his chin was more visible at that angle, and she recalled her mother's holding up a card when they were playing double solitaire once while waiting for him for dinner: "Looks like Daddy. . . ." "Let me see . . . sure does. . . ." She had seen the florid printed face often enough, the smile affable, the chin cleft. "Jack of Diamonds," her mother said. For hadn't the two of them also seen the father's face turn fixed and mysterious as the painted image, unchanging from whatever it had changed to? The same twice over: she hadn't thought that till now. He reached up and took her hand. The gesture seemed to say they had blundered into the fire once, but maybe never again.

The scent of pine, the essence of oak scent, too, came warm to her senses, assertive as animals. She rubbed with her free hand at the small debris that hugged the rock. In former times she had peeled away hunks of moss for bringing back. The rock was old enough to be dead, but in school they said that rocks lived.

"You're going to sell it, aren't you? The cottage, I mean."

"I have to. I need the money."

"I thought you were getting money, lots."

"I'm getting some. But not enough."

So he had laid an ace out before her. There was nothing to say. The returned silence, known to trees, rocks, and water, went agelessly on.

Nat Jennings sat up lightly, in one motion. "What mysteries attend my Rosalind, wandering through her forest of Arden?"

"I was chased by a bear," said Rosalind, attempting to joke with him, but remembering she had almost cried just now, she blew her nose on a torn Kleenex.

"Sleeping in his bed, were you? Serves you right."

He scratched his back where something bit. "I damned near fell asleep." He got to his feet. "It's time." It's what he'd said when they left that other time, three years ago. He put out his hand.

Pulling her up, he slipped on a mossy patch of rock and nearly fell. But dancing was in his bones; if he hadn't been good at it, they both would have fallen. As it was they clung and held upright.

Rosalind and her father got into the boat and paddled toward the cottage, keeping perfect time. Eva, not visible, was busy inside. They found her in the living room.

She had the red scarf wound about her head gypsy-fashion. Above her large glasses, it looked comical, but right; sexy and friendly, the way she was always being. She had cleared up everything from breakfast and was packing.

"You two looked like a picture coming in. I should have had a camera."

"Oh, we're a photogenic pair," Nat said.

"Were you ever tempted to study theater?" Eva asked her.

"I was, but— Not now. Oh, no, not now!" She stood apart, single, separate, ready to leave.

Startled by her tone, Nat Jennings turned. "I think it was her mother," he quickly said. "She didn't like the idea."

THE BUSINESS VENTURE

We were down at the river that night. Pete Owens was there with his young wife, Hope (his name for her was Jezzie, after Jezebel in the Bible), and Charlie and me, and both the Houston boys, one with his wife and the other with the latest in a string of new girlfriends. But Nelle Townshend, his steady girl, wasn't there.

We talked and watched the water flow. It was different from those nights we used to go up to the club and dance, because we were older and hadn't bothered to dress, just wore slacks and shorts. It was a clear night but no moon.

Even five years married to him, I was in love with Charlie more than ever, and took his hand to rub the reddish hairs around his wrist. I held his hand under water and watched the flow around it, and later when the others went up to the highway for more whiskey, we kissed like two high school kids and then waded out laughing and splashed water on each other.

The next day Pete Owens looked me up at the office when my boss, Mr. McGinnis, was gone to lunch. "Charlie's never quit, you know, Eileen. He's still passing favors out."

My heart dropped. I could guess it, but wasn't letting myself know I really knew it. I put my hard mask on. "What's the matter? Isn't Hope getting enough from you?"

"Oh, I'm the one for Jezzie. You're the main one for Charlie. I just mean, don't kid yourself he's ever stopped."

"When did any of us ever stop?"

"You have. You like him that much. But don't think you're home free. The funny thing is, nobody's ever took a shotgun to Charlie. So far's I know, nobody's ever even punched him in the jaw."

"It is odd," I said, sarcastic, but he didn't notice.

"It's downright peculiar," said Pete. "But then I guess we're a special sort of bunch, Eileen."

I went back to typing and wished he'd go. He'd be asking me next. We'd dated and done a few things, but that was so long ago, it didn't count now. It never really mattered. I never thought much about it.

"What I wonder is, Eileen. Is everybody else like us, or so different from us they don't know what we're like at all?"

"The world's changing," I said. "They're all getting like us."

"You mean it?"

I nodded. "The word got out," I said. "You told somebody, and they told somebody else, and now everybody is like us."

"Or soon will be," he said.

"That's right," I said.

I kept on typing letters, reeling them on and off the platen and working on my electric machine the whole time he was talking, turning his hat over and picking at a straw or two off the synthetic weave. I had a headache that got worse after he was gone.

Also at the picnic that night was Grey Houston, one of the Houston brothers, who was always with a different girl. His former steady girlfriend, Nelle Townshend, kept a cleaning and pressing shop on her own premises. Her mother had been a stay-at-home lady for years. They had one of those beautiful old Victorian-type houses—it just missed being a photographer's and tourist attraction, being about twenty years too late and having the wooden trim too ornate for the connoisseurs to call it the real classical style. Nelle had been enterprising enough to turn one wing of the house where nobody went anymore into a cleaning shop, because she needed to make some money and felt she had to be near her mother. She had working for them off and on a Negro back from the Vietnam war who had used his veterans' educational benefits to train as a dry cleaner. She picked up the idea when her mother happened to remark one night after she had paid him for some carpenter work, "Ain't that a dumb nigger, learning dry cleaning with nothing to dry-clean."

Now, when Mrs. Townshend said "nigger," it wasn't as if one of us had said it. She went back through the centuries for her words, back to when "ain't" was good grammar. "Nigger" for her just meant "black." But it was assuming Robin had done something dumb that was the mistake. Because he wasn't dumb, and Nelle knew it. He told her he'd applied for jobs all around, but they didn't offer much and he might have to go to Biloxi or Hattiesburg or Gulfport to get one. The trouble was, he owned a house here. Nelle said, "Maybe you could work for me."

He told her about a whole dry cleaning plant up in Magee that had folded up recently due to the old man who ran it dying on his feet one day. They drove up there together and she bought it. Her mother didn't like it much when she moved the equipment in, but Nelle did it anyway. "I never get the smell out of my hair," she would say, "but if it can just make money I'll get used to it." She was dating Grey at the time, and I thought that's what gave her that much nerve.

Grey was a darling man. He was divorced from a New Orleans woman, somebody with a lot of class and money. She'd been crazy about Grey, as who wouldn't be, but he didn't "fit in," was her complaint. "Why do I have to fit in with her?" he kept asking. "Why shouldn't she fit in with us?" "She was O.K. with us," I said. "Not quite," he said. "Y'all never did relax. You never felt easy. That's why Charlie kept working at her, flirting and all. She maybe ought to have gone ahead with Charlie. Then she'd have been one of us. But she acted serious about it. I said, 'Whatever you decide about Charlie, just don't tell me.' She was too serious."

"Anybody takes it seriously ought to be me," I said.

"Oh-oh," said Grey, breaking out with fun, the way he could do—in the depths one minute, up and laughing the next. "You can't afford that, Eileen."

That time I raised a storm at Charlie. "What did you want to get married for? You're nothing but a goddamn stud!"

"What's news about it?" Charlie wanted to know. "You're just getting worked up over nothing."

"Nothing! Is what we do just nothing?"

"That's right. When it's done with, it's nothing. What I think of you—now, that's something." He had had some problem with a new car at the garage—he had the GM agency then—and he smelled of clean lubricating products and new upholstery and the rough soap where the mechanics cleaned up. He was big and gleaming, the all-over male. Oh, hell, I thought, what can I do? Then, suddenly curious, I asked: "*Did* you make out with Grey's wife?"

He laughed out loud and gave me a sidelong kiss. "Now that's more like it."

Because he'd never tell me. He'd never tell me who he made out with. "Honey," he'd say, late at night in the dark, lying straight out beside me, occasionally tangling his toes in mine or reaching for his cigarettes, "if I'd say I never had another woman outside you, would you believe it?"

I couldn't say No from sheer astonishment.

"Because it just might be true," he went on in the dark, serious as a judge. Then I would start laughing, couldn't help it. Because there are few things in the world which you know are true. You don't know (not anymore: our mamas knew) if there's a God or not, much less if He so loved the world. You don't know what your own native land is up to, or the true meaning of freedom, or the real cost of gasoline and cigarettes, or whether your insurance company will pay up. But one thing I personally know that is *not* true is that Charlie Waybridge has had only one woman. Looked at that way, it can be a comfort, one thing to be sure of.

It was soon after the picnic on the river that Grey Houston came by to see me at the office. You'd think I had nothing to do but stop and talk. What he came about was Nelle.

"She won't date me anymore," he complained. "I thought we were doing fine, but she quit me just like that. Hell, I can't tell what's the trouble with her. I want to call up and say, 'Just tell me, Nelle. What's going on?' "

"Why don't you?" I asked.

Grey is always a little worried about things to do with people, especially since his divorce. We were glad when he started dating Nelle. She was hovering around thirty and didn't have anybody, and Grey was only a year or two younger.

"If I come right out and ask her, then she might just say, 'Let's decide to be good friends,' or something like that. Hell, I got enough friends."

"It's to be thought of," I agreed.

"What would you do?" he persisted.

"I'd rather know where I stand," I said, "but in this case I think I'd wait awhile. Nelle's worrying over that business. Maybe she doesn't know herself."

"I might push her too soon. I thought that, too."

"I ought to go around and see old Mrs. Townshend," I said. "She hardly gets out at all anymore. I mean to stop in and say hello."

"You're not going to repeat anything?"

See how he is? Skittery. "Of course not," I said. "But there's such a thing as keeping my eyes and ears open."

I went over to call on old Mrs. Townshend one Thursday afternoon when Mr. McGinnis's law office was closed anyway. The Townshend house is on a big lawn, a brick walk running up from the street to the front steps and a large round plot of elephant ears in the front yard. When away and thinking of home, I see right off the Townshend yard and the elephant ears.

I wasn't even to the steps before I smelled clothes just dry-cleaned. I don't guess it's so bad, though hardly what you'd think of living with. Nor would you particularly like to see the sign outside the porte-cochere, though way to the left of the walk and not visible from the front porch. Still, it was out there clearly, saying "Townshend Dry Cleaning: Rapid Service." Better than a funeral parlor, but not much.

The Townshend house is stuffed with things. All these little Victorian tables on tall legs bowed outward, a small lower shelf, and the top covered katy-corner with a clean starched linen doily, tatting around the edge. All these chairs of various shapes, especially one that rocked squeaking on a walnut stand, and for every chair a doily at the head. Mrs. Townshend kept two birdcages, but no birds were in them. There never had been any so far as I knew. It wasn't a dark house, though. Nelle had taken out the stained glass way back when she graduated from college. That was soon after her older sister married, and her mama needed her. "If I'm going to live here," she had said, "that's got to go." So it went.

Mrs. Townshend never raised much of a fuss at Nelle. She was low to the ground because of a humpback, a rather placid old lady. The Townshends were the sort to keep everything just the way it was. Mrs. Townshend was a LeMoyne from over toward Natchez. She was an Episcopalian and had brought her daughters up in that church.

"I'm sorry about this smell," she said in her forthright way, coming in and offering me a Coke on a little tray with a folded linen napkin beside it. "Nelle told me I'd get used to it and she was right: I have. But at first I had headaches all the time. If you get one I'll get some aspirin for you."

"How's the business going?" I asked.

"Nelle will be in in a minute. She knows you're here. You can ask her." She never raised her voice. She had a soft little face and gray eyes back of her little gold-rimmed glasses. She hadn't got to the hearing-aid stage yet, but you had to speak up. We went through the whole rigmarole of mine and Charlie's families. I had a feeling she was never much interested in all that, but around home you have to do it. Then I asked her what she was reading and she woke up. We got off the ground right away, and went strong about the President and foreign affairs, the picture not being so bright but of great interest, and about her books from the library always running out, and all the things she had against book clubs—then Nelle walked in.

Nelle Townshend doesn't look like anybody else but herself. Her face is like something done on purpose to use up all the fine skin, drawing it evenly over the bones beneath, so that no matter at what age, she always would look the same. But that day she had this pinched look I'd never seen before, and her arms were splotched with what must have been a reaction to the cleaning fluids. She rolled down the sleeves of her blouse and sat in an old wicker rocker.

"I saw Grey the other day, Nelle," I said. "I think he misses you."

She didn't say anything outside of remarking she hadn't much time to go out. Then she mentioned some sort of decorating at the church she wanted to borrow some ferns for, from the florist. He's got some he rents, in washtubs. "You can't get all those ferns in our little church," Mrs. Townshend said, and Nelle said she thought two would do. She'd send Robin, she said. Then the bell rang to announce another customer. Nelle had to go because Robin was at the "plant"—actually the old cook's house in back of the property where they'd set the machinery up.

I hadn't said all I had to say to Nelle, so when I got up to go, I said to Mrs. Townshend that I'd go in the office a minute on the way out. But Mrs. Townshend got to her feet, a surprise in itself. Her usual words were, You'll excuse me if I don't get up. Of course, you would excuse her and be too polite to ask why. Like a lot of old ladies, she might have arthritis. But this time she stood.

"I wish you'd let Nelle alone. Nelle is all right now. She's the way she wants to be. She'd not the way you people are. She's just not a bit that way!"

It may have been sheer surprise that kept me from telling Charlie all this till the weekend. We were hurrying to get to Pete and Hope Owens's place for a dinner they were having for some people down from the Delta, visitors.

"What did you say to that?" Charlie asked me.

"I was too surprised to open my mouth. I wouldn't have thought Mrs. Townshend would express such a low opinion as that. And why does she have it in the first place? Nelle's always been part of our crowd. She grew up with us. I thought they liked us."

"Old ladies get notions. They talk on the phone too much."

To our surprise, Nelle was at the Owenses' dinner, too. Hope told me in the kitchen that she'd asked her, and then asked Grey. But Grey had a date with the little Springer girl he'd brought to the picnic, Carole Springer. "If this keeps up," Hope said to me while I was helping her with a dip, "we're going to have a Springer in our crowd. I'm just not right ready for that." "Me either," I said. The Springers were from McComb, in lumber. They had money but they never were much fun.

"Did Nelle accept knowing you were going to ask Grey?" I asked.

"I couldn't tell that. She just said she'd love to and would come about seven."

It must have been seven, because Nelle walked in. "Can I help?"

"Your mama," I said, when Hope went out with the tray, "she sort of got upset with me the other day. I don't know why. If I said anything wrong, just tell her I'm sorry."

Nelle looked at her fresh nail polish. "Mama's a little peculiar now and then. Like everybody." So she wasn't about to open up.

"I've been feeling bad about Grey is all," I said. "You can think I'm meddling if you want to."

"Grey's all right," she said. "He's been going around with Carole Springer from McComb."

"All the more reason for feeling bad. Did you know they're coming tonight?"

She smiled a little distantly, and we went out to join the party. Charlie was already sitting up too close to the wife of the guest couple. I'd met them before. They have an antique shop. He is tall and nice, and she is short (wears spike heels) and nice. They are the sort you can't ever remember what their names are. If you get the first names right you're doing well. Shirley and Bob.

"Honey, you're just a doll," Charlie was saying (if he couldn't think of Shirley, Honey would do), and Pete said, "Watch out, Shirley, the next thing you know you'll be sitting on his lap."

"I almost went in for antiques myself," Nelle was saying to Bob, the husband. "I would have liked that better, of course, than a cleaning business, but I thought the turnover here would be too small. I do need to feel like I'm making money if I'm going to work at it. For a while, though, it was fun to go wandering around New Orleans and pick up good things cheap."

"I'd say they'd all been combed over down there," Bob objected.

"It's true about the best things," Nelle said. "I could hardly afford those anyway. But sometimes you see some pieces with really good design and you can see you might realize something on them. Real appreciation goes a long way."

"Bob has a jobber up in St. Louis," Shirley said. "We had enough of all this going around shaking the bushes. A few lucky finds was what got us started."

Nelle said, "I started thinking about it because I went in the living room a year or so back and there were some ladies I never saw before. They'd found the door open and walked in. They wanted to know the price of Mama's furniture. I said it wasn't for sale, but Mama was just coming in from the kitchen and heard them. You wouldn't believe how mad she got. 'I'm going straight and get out my pistol,' she said."

"You ought to just see her mama," said Hope. "This tiny little old lady."

"So what happened?" Shirley asked when she got through laughing.

"Nothing real bad," said Nelle. "They just got out the door as quick as they could."

"Yo' mama got a pistol?" Charlie asked, after a silence. We started to laugh again, the implication being plain that a Charlie Waybridge *needs* to know if a woman's mother has a pistol in the house.

"She does have one," said Nelle.

"So watch out, Charlie," said Pete.

Bob remarked, "Y'all certainly don't change much over here."

"Crazy as ever," Hope said proudly. It crossed my mind

that Hope was always protecting herself, one way or the other.

Shirley said she thought it was just grand to be back, she wouldn't take anything for it, and after that Grey and Carole arrived. We had another drink and then went in to dinner. Everybody acted like everything was okay. After dinner, I went back in the kitchen for some water, and there was Charlie, kissing Shirley. She was so strained up on tiptoe, Charlie being over six feet, that I thought, in addition to being embarrassed, mad, and backing out before they saw me, What they need is a stepladder to do it right.

On the way home, I told Charlie about catching them. "I didn't know she was within a country mile," he said, ready with excuses. "She just plain grabbed me."

"I've been disgusted once too often," I said. "Tell it to Bob."

"If she wanted to do it right," he said, "she ought to get a stepladder." So then I had to laugh. Even if our marriage wasn't ideal, we still had the same thoughts.

It sometimes seemed to me, in considering the crowd we were always part of, from even before we went to school, straight on through, that we were all like one person, walking around different ways, but in some permanent way breathing together, feeling the same reactions, thinking each other's thoughts. What do you call that if not love? If asked, we'd all cry Yes! with one voice, but then it's not our habit to ask anything serious. We're close to religious about keeping everything light and gay. Nelle Townshend knew that, all the above, but she was drawing back. A betrayer was what she was turning into. We felt weakened because of her. What did she think she was doing?

I had to drive Mr. McGinnis way back in the woods one day to serve a subpoena on a witness. He hadn't liked to drive since his heart attack, and his usual colored man was busy with Mrs. McGinnis's garden. In the course of that little trip, coming back into town, I saw Nelle Townshend's station wagon turn off onto a side road. I couldn't see who was with her, but somebody was, definitely.

I must add that this was spring and there were drifts of dogwood all mingled in the woods at different levels. Through those same woods, along the winding roads, the redbud, simultaneous, was spreading its wonderful pink haze. Mr. McGinnis sat beside me without saying much, his old knobby hands folded over a briefcase he held upright on his lap. "A trip like this just makes me think, Eileen, that everybody owes it to himself to get out in the woods this time of year. It's just God's own garden," he said. We had just crossed a wooden bridge over a pretty little creek about a mile back. That same creek, shallower, was crossed by a ford along the road that Nelle's car had taken. I know that little road, too, maybe the prettiest one of all.

Serpents have a taste for Eden, and in a small town, if they are busy elsewhere, lots of people are glad to fill in for them. It still upsets me to think of all the gossip that went on that year, and at the same time I have to blame Nelle Townshend for it, not so much for starting it, but for being so unconscious about it. She had stepped out of line and she didn't even bother to notice.

Once the business got going, the next thing she did was enroll in a class—a "seminar," she said—over at the university at Hattiesburg. It was something to do with art theory, she said, and she was thinking of going on from there to a degree, eventually, and get hold of a subject she could teach at the junior college right up the road. So settling in to be an old maid.

I said this last rather gloomily to Pete's wife, Hope, and Pete overheard and said, "There's all kinds of those." "You stop that," said Hope. "What's supposed to be going on?" I asked. (Some say don't ask, it's better not to, but I think you have to know if only to keep on guard.)

"Just that they're saying things about Nelle and that black Robin works for her."

"Well, they're in the same business," I said.

"Whatever it is, people don't like it. They say she goes out to his house after dark. That they spend too much time over the books."

"Somebody ought to warn her," I said. "If Robin gets into trouble she won't find anybody to do that kind of work. He's the only one."

"Nelle's gotten too independent is the thing," said Pete. "She thinks she can live her own life."

"Maybe she can," said Hope.

Charlie was away that week. He had gone over to the Delta on business, and Hope and Pete had dropped in to keep me company. Hope is ten years younger than Pete. (Pete used to date her sister, Mary Ruth, one of these beauty-queen types, who had gone up to the Miss America pageant to represent Mississippi and come back first runner-up. For the talent contest part of it, she had recited passages from the Bible, and Pete always said her trouble was she was too religious but he hoped to get her over it. She used to try in a nice way to get him into church work, and that embarrassed him. It's our common habit, as Mary Ruth well knew, to go to morning service, but anything outside that is out. Anyway, around Mary Ruth's he used to keep seeing the little sister Hope, and he'd say, "Mary Ruth, you better start on that girl about church, she's growing up dynamite." Mary Ruth got involved in a promotion trip, something about getting right with America, and met a man on a plane trip to Dallas, and before the seat-belt sign went off they were in love. For Mary Ruth that meant marriage. She was strict, a woman of faith, and I don't think Pete would have been happy with her. But he had got the habit of the house by then, and Mary Ruth's parents had got fond of him and didn't want him drinking too much: they made him welcome. So one day Hope turned seventeen and came out in a new flouncy dress with heels on, and Pete saw the light.)

We had a saying by now that Pete had always been younger than Hope, that she was older than any of us. Only twenty, she worked at making their house look good and won gardening prizes. She gave grand parties, with attention to details.

"I stuck my neck out," I told Hope, "to keep Nelle dating Grey. You remember her mama took a set at me like I never dreamed possible. Nelle's been doing us all funny, but she may have to come back someday. We can't stop caring for her."

Hope thought it over. "Robin knows what it's like here, even if Nelle may have temporarily forgotten. He's not going to tempt fate. Anyway, somebody already spoke to Nelle."

"Who?"

"Grey, of course. He'll use any excuse to speak to her. She got mad as a firecracker. She said, 'Don't you know this is nineteen seventy-*six*? I've got a business to run. I've got a living to make!' But she quit going out to his house at night. And Robin quit so much as answering the phone, up at her office."

"You mean he's keeping one of those low profiles?" said Pete.

Soon after, I ran into Robin uptown in the grocery, and he said, "How do you do, Mrs. Waybridge," like a schoolteacher or a foreigner, and I figured just from that, that he was on to everything and taking no chances. Nelle must have told him. I personally knew what not many people did, that he was a real partner with Nelle, not just her hired help. They had got Mr. McGinnis to draw up the papers. And they had plans for moving the plant uptown, to an empty store building, with some investment in more equipment. So maybe they'd get by till then. I felt a mellowness in my heart about Nelle's effort and all—a Townshend (LeMoyne on her mother's side) opening a dry cleaning business. I thought of Robin's effort, too—he had a sincere, intelligent look, reserved. What I hoped for them was something like a prayer.

Busying my thoughts about all this, I had been forgetting Charlie. That will never do.

For one thing, leaving aside women, Charlie's present way of life was very nearly wild. He'd got into oil leases two years before, and when something was going on, he'd drive like a demon over to East Texas by way of Shreveport and back through Pike and Amite counties. At one time he had to sit over Mr. McGinnis for a month getting him to study up on laws governing oil rights. In the end, Charlie got to know as much or more than Mr. McGinnis. He's in and out. The in-between times are when he gets restless. Drinks too much and starts simmering up about some new woman. One thing (except for me), with Charlie it's always a new woman. Once tried, soon dropped. Or so I like to believe. Then, truth to tell, there is really part of me that not only wants to believe but at unstated times does believe that I've been the only one for Charlie Waybridge. Not that I'd begrudge him a few times of having it off down in the hollow back of the gym with some girl who came in from the country, nor would I think anything about flings in New Orleans while he was in Tulane. But as for the outlandish reputation he's acquired now, sometimes I just want to say out loud to all and sundry, "There's not a word of truth in it. He's a big, attractive, friendly guy, O.K.! But he's not the town stud. He belongs to *me*."

All this before the evening along about first dark when Charlie was seen on the Townshend property by Nelle's mother, who went and got the pistol and shot at him.

"Christ, she could have killed me," Charlie said. He was

too surprised about it even to shake. He was just dazed. Fixed a stiff drink and didn't want any supper. "She's gone off her rocker," he said. "That's all I could think."

I knew I had to ask it, sooner or later. "What were you doing up there, Charlie?"

"Nothing," he said. "I'd left the car at Wharton's garage to check why I'm burning too much oil. He's getting to it in the morning. It was a nice evening and I cut through the back alley and that led to a stroll through the Townshend pasture. That's all. I saw the little lady out on the back porch. I was too far off to holler at her. She scuttled off into the house and I was going past, when here she came out again with something black weighting her hand. You know what I thought? I thought she had a kitten by the neck. Next thing I knew there was a bullet smashing through the leaves not that far off." He put his hand out.

"Wonder if Nelle was home."

I was nervous as a monkey after I heard this, and nothing would do me but to call up Nelle.

She answered right away. "Nelle," I said, "is your little mama going in for target practice these days?"

She started laughing. "Did you hear that all the way to your place? She's mad 'cause the Johnsons' old cow keeps breaking down our fence. She took a shot in the air because she's tired complaining."

"Since when was Charlie Waybridge a cow?" I asked.

"Mercy, Eileen. You don't mean Charlie was back there?"

"You better load that thing with blanks," I said, "or hide it."

"Blanks is all it's got in it," said Nelle. "Mama doesn't tell that because she feels more protected not to."

"You certainly better check it out," I said. "Charlie says it was a bullet."

There was a pause. "You're not mad or anything, are you, Eileen?"

"Oh, no," I warbled. "We've been friends too long for that."

"Come over and see us," said Nelle. "Real soon."

I don't know who told it, but knowing this town like the back of my hand, I know *how* they told it. Charlie Waybridge was up at Nelle Townshend's and old Mrs. Townshend shot at him. Enough said. At the Garden Club Auxiliary tea, I came in and heard them giggling, and how they got quiet when I passed a plate of sandwiches. I went straight to the subject, which is the way I do. "Y'all off on Mrs. Townshend?" I asked. There was a silence, and then some little cross-eyed bride, new in town, piped up that there was just always something funny going on here, and Maud Varner, an old friend, said she thought Nelle ought to watch out for Mrs. Townshend, she was showing her age. "It's not such a funny goings-on when it almost kills somebody," I said. "Charlie came straight home and told me. He was glad to be alive, but I went and called Nelle. So she does know." There was another silence during which I could tell what everybody thought. The thing is not to get too distant or above it all. If you do, your friends will pull back, too, and you won't know anything. Gradually, you'll just turn into, Poor Eileen, what does she think of all Charlie's carryings-on?

Next, the injunction. Who brought it and why? I got the answer to the first before I guessed the second.

It was against the Townshend Cleaners because the chemicals used were a hazard to health and the smell they exuded a public nuisance. But the real reason wasn't this at all.

In order to speed up the deliveries, Nelle had taken to driving the station wagon herself, so that Robin could run in with the cleaning. Some people had begun to remark on this. Would it have been different if Nelle was married or had a brother, a father, a steady boyfriend? I don't know. I used to hold my breath when they went by in the late afternoon together. Because sometimes when the back of the station-wagon was full, Robin would be up on the front seat with her, and she with her head stuck in the air, driving carefully, her mind on nothing at all to do with other people. Once the cleaning load got lighter, Robin would usually sit on the back seat, as expected to do. But sometimes, busy talking to her, he wouldn't. He'd be up beside her, discussing business.

Then, suddenly, the business closed.

Nelle was beside herself. She came running to Mr. McGinnis. Her hair was every which way around her head and she was wearing an old checked shirt and no makeup.

She could hardly make herself sit still and visit with me while Mr. McGinnis got through with a client. "Now, Miss Nelle," he said, steering her through the door.

"Just when we were making a go of it!" I heard her say; then he closed the door.

I heard by way of the grapevine that very night that the person who had done it was John Houston, Grey's brother, whose wife's family lived on a property just below the Townshends. They claimed they couldn't sleep for the dry-cleaning fumes and were getting violent attacks of nausea.

"Aren't they supposed to give warnings?" I asked.

We were all at John and Rose Houston's home, a real gathering of the bunch, only Nelle being absent, though she was the most present one of all. There was a silence after every statement, in itself unusual. Finally John Houston said, "Not in cases of extreme health hazard."

"That's a lot of you-know-what," I said. "Rose, your family's not dying."

Rose said: "They never claimed to be dying." And Pete said: "Eileen, can't you sit right quiet and try to use your head?"

"In preference to running off at the mouth," said Charlie, which made me mad. I was refusing, I well knew, to see the point they all had in mind. But it seemed to me that was my privilege.

The thing to know about our crowd is that we never did go in for talking about the "Negro question." We talked about Negroes the way we always had, like people, one at a time. They were all around us, had always been, living around us, waiting on us, sharing our lives, brought up with us, nursing us, cooking for us, mourning and rejoicing with us, making us laugh, stealing from us, digging our graves. But when all the troubles started coming in on us after the Freedom Riders and the Ole Miss riots, we decided not to talk about it. I don't know but what we weren't afraid of getting nervous. We couldn't jump out of our own skins, or those of our parents, grandparents, and those before them. "Nothing you can do about it" was Charlie's view. "Whatever you decide, you're going to act the same way tomorrow as you did today. Hoping you can get Alma to cook for you, and Peabody to clean the windows, and Bayman to cut the grass." "I'm not keeping anybody from voting—yellow, blue, or pink," said Hope, who had got her "ideas" straight from the first, she said. "I don't guess any of us is," said Pete, "them days is gone forever." "But wouldn't it just be wonderful," said Rose Houston, "to have a little colored gal to pick up your handkerchief and sew on your buttons and bring you cold lemonade and fan you when you're hot, and just love you to death?"

Rose was joking, of course, the way we all liked to do. But there are always one or two of them that we seriously insist we know—really *know*—that they love us. Would do anything for us, as we would for them. Otherwise, without that feeling, I guess we couldn't rest easy. You never can really know what they think, what they feel, so there's always the one chance it might be love.

So we—the we I'm always speaking of—decided not to

talk about race relations because it spoiled things too much. We didn't like to consider anyone of us really involved in some part of it. Then, in my mind's eye, I saw Nelle's car, that dogwood-laden day in the woods, headed off the road with somebody inside. Or such was my impression. I'd never mentioned it to anybody, and Mr. McGinnis hadn't, I think, seen. Was it Robin? Or maybe, I suddenly asked myself, Charlie? Mysteries multiplied.

"Nelle's got to make a living is the whole thing," said Pete, getting practical. "We can't not let her do that,"

"Why doesn't somebody find her a job she'd like?" asked Grey.

"Why the hell," Charlie burst out, "don't you marry her, Grey? Women ought to get married," he announced in general. "You see what happens when they don't."

"Hell, I can't get near her," said Grey. "We dated for six months. I guess I wasn't the one," he added.

"She ought to relocate the plant uptown, then she could run the office in her house, one remove from it, acting like a lady."

"What about Robin?" said Hope.

"He could run back and forth," I said. "They do want to do that," I added, "but can't afford it yet."

"You'd think old Mrs. Townshend would have stopped it all."

"That lady's a mystery."

"If Nelle just had a brother."

"Or even an uncle."

Then the talk dwindled down to silence.

"John," said Pete, after a time, turning around to face him, "we all know it was you—not Rose's folks. Did you have to?"

John Houston was sitting quietly in his chair. He was a little older than the rest of us, turning gray, a little more settled and methodical, more like our uncle than an equal and friend. (Or was it just that he and Rose were the only ones so far to have children—what all our parents said we all ought to do, but couldn't quit having our good times.) He was sipping bourbon. He nodded slowly. "I had to." We didn't ask any more.

"Let's just go quiet," John finally added. "Wait and see."

Now, all my life I'd been hearing first one person then another (and these, it would seem, appointed by silent consensus) say that things were to be taken care of in a certain way and no other. The person in this case who had this kind of appointment was evidently John Houston, from in our midst. But when did he get it? How did he get it? Where did it come from? There seemed to be no need to discuss it.

Rose Houston, who wore her long light hair in a sort of loose bun at the nape and who sat straight up in her chair, adjusted a fallen strand, and Grey went off to fix another drink for himself and Pete and Hope. He sang on the way out, more or less to himself, "For the times they are a-changing . . ." and that, too, found reference in all our minds. Except I couldn't help but wonder whether anything had changed at all.

The hearing on the dry cleaning injunction was due to be held in two weeks. Nelle went off to the coast. She couldn't stand the tension, she told me, having come over to Mr. McGinnis's office to see him alone. "Thinking how we've worked and all," she said, "and how just before this came up the auditor was in and told us what good shape we were in. We were just about to buy a new condenser."

"What's that?" I asked.

"Takes the smell out of the fumes," she said. "The very thing they're mad about. I could kill John Houston. Why couldn't he have come to me?"

I decided to be forthright. "Nelle, there's something you ought to evaluate . . . consider, I mean. Whatever word you want." I was shaking, surprising myself.

Nobody was around. Mr. McGinnis was in the next county.

Once when I was visiting a school friend up north, out from Philadelphia, a man at a party asked me if I would have sexual relations with a black. He wasn't black himself, so why was he curious? I said I'd never even thought about it. "It's a taboo, I think you call it," I said. "Girls like me get brainwashed early on. It's not that I'm against them," I added, feeling awkward. "Contrary to what you may think or may even believe," he told me, "you've probably thought a lot about it. You've suppressed your impulses, that's all." "Nobody can prove that," I said, "not even you," I added, thinking I was being amusing. But he only looked superior and walked away.

"It's you and Robin," I said. I could hear myself explaining to Charlie, Somebody had to, sooner or later. "You won't find anybody really believing anything, I don't guess, but it's making people speculate."

Nelle Townshend never reacted the way you'd think she would. She didn't even get annoyed, much less hit the ceiling. She just gave a little sigh. "You start a business, you'll see. I've got no time for anything but worrying about customers and money."

I was wondering whether to tell her the latest. A woman named McCorkle from out in the country, who resembled Nelle so much from the back you'd think they were the same, got pushed off the sidewalk last Saturday and fell in the concrete gutter up near the drugstore. The person who did it, somebody from outside town, must have said something nobody heard but Mrs. McCorkle, because she jumped up with her skirt muddy and stockings torn and yelled out, "I ain't no nigger lover!"

But I didn't tell her. If she was anybody but a Townshend,

I might have. Odd to think that, when the only Townshends left there were Nelle and her mother. In cases such as this, the absent are present and the dead are, too. Mr. Townshend had died so long ago you had to ask your parents what he was like. The answer was always the same. "Sid Townshend was a mighty good man." Nelle had had two sisters: one died in her twenties, the victim of a rare disease, and the other got married and went to live on a place out from Helena, Arkansas. She had about six children and could be of no real help to the home branch.

"Come over to dinner," I coaxed. "You want me to ask Grey, I will. If you don't, I won't."

"Grey," she said, just blank, like that. He might have been somebody she met once a long time back. "She's a perpetual virgin," I heard Charlie say once. "Just because she won't cotton up to you," I said. But maybe he was right. Nelle and her mother lived up near the Episcopal church. Since our little town could not support a full-time rector, it was they who kept the church linens and the chalice and saw that the robes were always cleaned and hung in their proper place in the little room off the chancel. Come to think of it, keeping those robes and surplices in order may have been one thing that started Nelle into dry cleaning.

Nelle got up suddenly, her face catching the light from our old window with the wobbly glass in the panes, and I thought, She's a grand-looking woman, sort of girlish and womanish both.

"I'm going to the coast," she said. "I'm taking some books and a sketch pad. I may look into some art courses. You have to have training to teach anything, that's the trouble."

"Look, Nelle, if it's money— Well, you do have friends, you know."

"Friends," she said, just the way she had said "Grey." I wondered just what Nelle was really like. None of us seemed to know.

"Have a good time," I said. After she left, I thought I heard the echo of that blank, soft voice saying, "Good time."

It was a week after Nelle had gone that old Mrs. Townshend rang up Mr. McGinnis at the office. Mr. McGinnis came out to tell me what it was all about.

"Mrs. Townshend says that last night somebody tore down the dry cleaning sign Nelle had put up out at the side. Some colored woman is staying with her at night, but neither one of them saw anybody. Now she can't find Robin to put it back. She's called his house but he's not there."

"Do they say he'll be back soon?"

"They say he's out of town."

"I'd get Charlie to go up and fix it, but you know what happened."

"I heard about it. Maybe in daylight the old lady won't shoot. I'll go around with our yardman after dinner." What we still mean by dinner is lunch. So they put the sign up and I sat in the empty office wondering about this and that, but mainly, Where was Robin Byers?

It's time to say that Robin Byers was not any Harry Belafonte calypso-singing sex symbol of a "black." He was strong and thoughtful-looking, not very tall, definitely chocolate, but not ebony. He wore his hair cropped short in an almost military fashion so that, being thick, it stuck straight up more often than not. From one side he could look positively frightening, as he had a long white scar running down the side of his cheek. It was said that he got it in the army, in Vietnam, but the story of just how was not known. So maybe he had not gotten it in the war, but somewhere else. His folks had been in the county forever, his own house being not far out from town. He had a wife, two teenaged children, a telephone, and a TV set. The other side of Robin Byers's face was regular, smooth, and while not especially handsome it was good-humored and likable. All in all, he looked intelligent and conscientious, and that must have been how Nelle Townshend saw him, as he was.

I went to the hearing. I'd have had to, to keep Mr. McGinnis's notes straight, but I would have anyway, as all our crowd showed up, except Rose and John Houston. Rose's parents were there, having brought the complaint, and Rose's mama's doctor from over at Hattiesburg, to swear she'd had no end of allergies and migraines, and attacks of nausea, all brought on by the cleaning fumes. Sitting way in the back was Robin Byers, in a suit (a really nice suit) with a blue-and-white-striped "city" shirt and a knit tie. He looked like an assistant university dean, except for the white scar. He also had the look of a spectator, very calm, I thought, not wanting to keep turning around and staring at him, but keeping the image in my mind like an all-day sucker, letting it slowly melt out its meaning. He was holding a certain surface. But he was scared. Half across the courtroom you could see his temple throbbing, and the sweat beads. He was that tense. The whole effect was amazing.

The complaint was read out and Mrs. Hammond, Rose's mother, testified and the doctor testified, and Mr. Hammond said they were both right. The way the Hammonds talk—big Presbyterians—you would think they had the Bible on their side every minute, so naturally everybody else had to be mistaken. Friends and neighbors of the Townshends all these years, they now seemed to be speaking of people they knew only slightly. That is until Mrs. Hammond, a sort of dumpling-like woman with a practiced way of sounding accurate about whatever she said (she was a good gossip because she got all the details of everything), suddenly came down to a personal level and said, "Nelle, I just don't see why if you want to run that thing you don't move it into town," and Nelle said back right away just like they were in a living room instead of a courthouse, "Well, that's because of Mama, Miss

Addie. This way I'm in and out with her." At that, everybody laughed, couldn't help it.

Then Mr. McGinnis got up and challenged that very much about Mrs. Hammond's headaches and allergies (he established her age, fifty-two, which she didn't want to tell) had to do with the cleaning plant. If they had, somebody else would have such complaints, but in case we needed to go further into it, he would ask Miss Nelle to explain what he meant.

Nelle got up front and went about as far as she could concerning the type of equipment she used and how it was guaranteed against the very thing now being complained of, that it let very few vapors escape, but then she said she would rather call on Robin Byers to come and explain because he had had special training in the chemical processes and knew all their possible negative effects.

And he came. He walked down the aisle and sat in the chair and nobody had ever seen such composure. I think he was petrified, but so might an actor be who was doing a role to high perfection. And when he started to talk you'd think that dry cleaning was a text and that his God-appointed task was to preach a sermon on it. But it wasn't quite like that, either. More modern. A professor giving a lecture to extremely ignorant students, with a good professor's accuracy, to the last degree. In the first place, he said, the cleaning fluid used was not varsol or carbon tetrachloride, which were known not only to give off harmful fumes but to damage fabrics, but something called "Perluxe" or perchlorethylene (he paused to give the chemical composition), which was approved for commercial cleaning purposes in such and such a solution by federal and state bylaws, of certain numbers and codes, which Mr. McGinnis had listed in his records and would be glad to read aloud upon request. If an operator worked closely with Perluxe for a certain number of hours a day, he might have headaches, it was true, but escaping vapor could scarcely be smelled at all more than a few feet from the exhaust pipes, and caused no harmful effects whatsoever, even to shrubs or "the leaves upon the trees." He said this last in such a lofty, rhythmic way that somebody giggled (I think it was Hope), and he stopped talking altogether.

"There might be smells down in those hollows back there," Nelle filled in from where she was sitting, "but it's not from my one little exhaust pipe."

"Then why," asked Mrs. Hammond right out, "do you keep on saying you need new equipment so you won't have any exhaust? Just answer me that."

"I'll let Robin explain," said Nelle.

"The fact is that Perluxe is an expensive product," Robin said. "At four dollars and twenty-five cents a gallon, using nearly thirty gallons each time the accumulation of the garments is put through the process, she can count on it that the overheads with two cleanings a week will run in the neighborhood of between two and three hundred dollars. So having the condenser machine would mean that the exhaust runs into it, and so converts the vapors back to the liquid, in order to use it once again."

"It's not for the neighbors," Nelle put in. "It's for us."

Everybody had spoken out of order by then, but what with the atmosphere having either declined or improved (depending on how you looked at it) to one of friendly inquiry among neighbors rather than a squabble in a court of law, the silence that finally descended was more meditative than not, having as its most impressive features, like high points in a landscape, Nelle, at some little distance down a front bench, but turned around so as to take everything in, her back straight and her Townshend head both superior and interested; and Robin Byers, who still had the chair by Judge Purvis's desk, collected and severe (he had forgotten the giggle), with testimony faultlessly delivered and nothing more he needed to say. (Would things have been any different if Charlie had been there? He was out of town.)

The judge cleared his throat and said he guessed the smells in the gullies around Tyler might be a nuisance, sure enough, but couldn't be said to be caused by dry cleaning, and he thought Miss Townshend could go on with her business. For a while, the white face and the black one seemed just the same, to be rising up quiet and superior above us all.

The judge asked, just out of curiosity, when Nelle planned to buy the condenser that was mentioned. She said whenever she could find one secondhand in good condition—they cost nearly two thousand dollars new—and Robin Byers put in that he had just been looking into one down in Biloxi, so it might not be too long. Biloxi is on the coast.

Judge Purvis said we'd adjourn now, and everybody stood up of one accord, except Mr. McGinnis, who had dozed off and was almost snoring.

Nelle, who was feeling friendly to the world, or seeming to (we all had clothes that got dirty, after all), said to all and sundry not to worry, "we plan to move the plant uptown one of these days before too long," and it was the "we" that came through again, a slip: she usually referred to the business as hers. It was just a reminder of what everybody wanted not to have to think about, and she probably hadn't intended to speak of it that way.

As if to smooth it well into the past, Judge Purvis remarked that these little towns ought to have zoning laws, but I sat there thinking there wouldn't be much support for that, not with the Gulf Oil station and garage right up on South Street between the Whitmans' and the Binghams', and the small-appliance shop on the vacant lot where the old Marshall mansion had stood, and the Tackett house, still elegant as you please, doing steady business as a funeral home. You can separate black from white but not business from nonbusiness. Not in our town.

Nelle came down and shook hands with Mr. McGinnis. "I don't know when I can afford to pay you." "Court costs go to them," he said. "Don't worry about the rest."

Back at the office, Mr. McGinnis closed the street door and said to me, "The fumes in this case have got nothing to do with dry cleaning. Has anybody talked to Miss Nelle?"

"They have," I said, "but she doesn't seem to pay any attention."

He said I could go home for the day and much obliged for my help at the courthouse. I powdered my nose and went out into the street. It wasn't but eleven-thirty.

Everything was still, and nobody around. The blue jays were having a good time on the courthouse yard, squalling and swooping from the lowest oak limbs, close to the ground, then mounting back up. There were some sparrows out near the old horse trough, which still ran water. They were splashing around. But except for somebody driving up for the mail at the post office, then driving off, there wasn't a soul around. I started walking, and just automatically I went by for the mail because as a rule Charlie didn't stop in for it till noon, even when in town. On the way I was mulling over the hearing and how Mrs. Hammond had said at the door of the courtroom to Nelle, "Aw right, Miss Nellie, you just wait." It wasn't said in any unpleasant way; in fact, it sounded right friendly. Except that she wasn't looking at Nelle, but past her, and except that being older, it wasn't the ordinary thing to call her "Miss," and except that Nelle is a pretty name but Nellie isn't. But Nelle in reply had suddenly laughed in that unexpected but delightful way she has, because something has struck her as really funny. "What am I supposed to wait *for,* Miss Addie?" Whatever else, Nelle wasn't scared. I looked for Robin Byers, but he had got sensible and gone off in that old little blue German car he drives. I saw Nelle drive home alone.

Then, because the lay of my home direction was a shortcut from the post office, and because the spring had been dry and the back lanes nice to walk in, I went through the same way Charlie had that time Mrs. Townshend had about killed him, and enjoyed, the way I had from childhood on, the soft fragrances of springtime, the brown wisps of spent jonquils withered on their stalks, the forsythia turned from yellow to green fronds, but the spirea still white as a bride's veil worked in blossoms, and the climbing roses, mainly wild, just opening a delicate, simple pink bloom all along the back fences. I was crossing down that way when what I saw was a blue car.

It was stopped way back down the Townshend property on a little connecting road that made an entrance through to a lower town road, one that nobody used anymore. I stopped in the clump of bowdarc trees on the next property from the Townshends'. Then I saw Nelle, running down the hill. She still had that same laugh, honest and joyous, that she had shown the first of to Mrs. Hammond. And there coming to meet her was Robin, his teeth white as his scar. They grabbed each other's hands, black on white and white on black. They started whirling each other around, like two schoolchildren in a game, and I saw Nelle's mouth forming the words I could scarcely hear: "We won! We won!" And his, the same, a baritone underneath. It was pure joy. Washing the color out, saying that the dye didn't, this time, hold, they could have been brother and sister, happy at some good family news, or old lovers (Charlie and I sometimes meet like that, too happy at some piece of luck to really stop to talk about it, just dancing out our joy). But, my God, I thought, don't they know they're black and white and this is Tyler, Mississippi? Well, of course they do, I thought next—that's more than half the joy—getting away with it! Dare and double-dare! Dumbfounded, I just stood, hidden, never seen by them at all, and let the image of black on white and white on black—

those pale, aristocratic Townshend hands and his strong, square-cut black ones—linked perpetually now in my mind's eye—soak in.

It's going to stay with me forever, I thought, but what does it mean? I never told. I didn't think they were lovers. But they were into a triumph of the sort that lovers feel. They had acted as they pleased. They were above everything. They lived in another world because of a dry cleaning business. They had proved it when they had to. They knew it.

But nobody could be counted on to see it the way I did. It was too complicated for any two people to know about it.

Soon after this we got a call from Hope, Pete's wife. "I've got tired of all this foolishness," she said. "How did we ever get hung up on dry cleaning, of all things? Can you feature it? I'm going to give a party. Mary Foote Williams is coming home to see her folks and bringing Keith, so that's good enough for me. And don't kid yourself. I'm personally going to get Nelle Townshend to come, and Grey Houston is going to bring her. I'm getting good and ready for everybody to start acting normal again. I don't know what's been the matter with everybody, and furthermore I don't want to know."

Well, this is a kettle of fish, I thought: Hope, the youngest, taking us over. Of course, she did have the perspective to see everything whole.

I no sooner put down the phone than Pete called up from his office. "Jezzie's on the warpath," he said. (He calls her Jezzie because she used to tell all kinds of lies to some little high school boy she had crazy about her—her own age—just so she could go out with Pete and the older crowd. It was easy to see through that. She thought she might just be getting a short run with us and would have to fall back on her own bunch when we shoved her out, so she was keeping a foothold. Pete caught her at it, but all it did was make him like her better. Hope was pert. She had a sharp little chin she liked to stick up in the air, and a turned-up nose. "Both signs of meanness," said Mr. Owens, Pete's father, "especially the nose," and buried his own in the newspaper.)

"Well," I said doubtfully, "if you think it's a good idea . . ."

"No stopping her," said Pete, with the voice of a spectator at the game. "If anybody can swing it, she can."

So we finally said yes.

The morning of Hope's party there was some ugly weather, one nasty little black cloud after another and a lot of restless crosswinds. There was a tornado watch out for our county and two others, making you know it was a widespread weather system. I had promised to bring a platter of shrimp for the buffet table, and that meant a whole morning shucking them after driving out to pick up the order at the Fish Shack. At times the lightning was popping so close I had to get out of the kitchen. I would go sit in the living room with the thunder blamming so hard I couldn't even read the paper. Looking out at my backyard through the picture window, the colors of the marigolds and pansies seemed to be electric bright, blazing, then shuddering in the wind.

I was bound to connect all this with the anxiety that had got into things about that party. Charlie's being over in Louisiana didn't help. Maybe all was calm and bright over there, but I doubted it.

However, along about two the sky did clear, and the sun came out. When I drove out to Hope and Pete's place with the shrimp—it's a little way north of town, reached by its own side road, on a hill—everything was wonderful. There was a warm buoyancy in the air that made you feel young and remember what it was like to skip home from school.

"It's cleared off," said Hope, as though in personal triumph over Nature.

Pete was behind her at the door, enveloped in a huge apron. "I feel like playing softball," he said.

"Me, too," I agreed. "If I could just hear from Charlie."

"Oh, he'll be back," said Pete. "Charlie miss a party? Never!"

Well, it was quite an affair. The effort was to get us all launched in a new and happy period and the method was the tried and true one of drinking and feasting, dancing, pranking, laughing, flirting, and having fun. I had a new knife-pleated silk skirt, ankle length, dark blue shot with green and cyclamen, and a new off-the-shoulder blouse, and Mary Foote Williams, the visitor, wore a slit skirt, but Hope took the cake in her hoop skirts from her senior-high-school days, and her hair in a coarse gold net.

"The shrimp are gorgeous," she said. "Come look. I called Mama and requested prayer for good weather. It never fails."

"Charlie called," I said. "He said he'd be maybe thirty minutes late and would come on his own."

A car pulled up in the drive and there was Grey circling around and holding the door for Nelle herself. She had on a simple silk dress with her fine hair brushed loose and a pair of sexy new high-heeled sandals. It looked natural to see them together and I breathed easier without knowing I hadn't been doing it for quite a while. Hope was right, we'd had enough of all this foolishness.

"That just leaves John and Rose," said Hope, "and I have my own ideas about them."

"What?" I asked.

"Well, I shouldn't say. It's y'all's crowd." She was quick in her kitchen, clicking around with her skirts swaying. She had got a nice little colored girl, Perline, dressed up in black with a white ruffled apron. "I just think John's halfway to a stuffed shirt and Rose is going to get him all the way there."

So, our crowd or not, she was going right ahead.

"I think this has to do with you-know-what," I said.

"We aren't going to mention you-know-what," said Hope.

"From now on, honey, my only four-letter words are 'dry' and 'cleaning.' "

John and Rose didn't show up, but two new couples did, a pair from Hattiesburg and the Kellmans, new in town but promising. Hope had let them in. Pete exercised himself at the bar and there was a strong punch as well. We strolled out to the pool and sat on white-painted iron chairs with cushions in green flowered plastic. Nelle sat with her pretty legs crossed, talking to Mary Foote. Grey was at her elbow. The little maid passed out canapés and shrimp. Light was still lingering in a clear sky barely pink at the edges. Pete skimmed leaves from the pool surface with a long-handled net. Lightning bugs winked and drifted, and the new little wife from Hattiesburg caught one or two in her palm and watched them crawl away, then take wing. "I used to do that," said Nelle. Then she shivered and Grey went for a shawl. It grew suddenly darker and one or two pale stars could be seen, then dozens. Pete, vanished inside, had started some records. Some people began to trail back in. And with another drink (the third, maybe?), it wasn't clear how much time had passed, when there came the harsh roar of a motor from the private road, growing stronger the nearer it got, a slashing of gravel in the drive out front, and a door slamming. And the first thing you knew there was Charlie Waybridge, filling the whole doorframe before Pete or Hope could even go to open it. He put his arms out to everybody. "Well, whaddaya know!" he said.

His tie was loose two buttons down and his light seersucker dress coat was crumpled and open but at least he had it on. I went right to him. He'd been drinking, of course, I'd known it from the first sound of the car—but who wasn't drinking? "Hi ya, baby!" he said, and grabbed me.

Then Pete and Hope were getting their greetings and were leading him up to meet the new people, till he got to the bar, where he dropped off to help himself.

It was that minute that Perline, the little maid, came in with a plate in her hand. Charlie swaggered up to her and said, "Well, if it ain't Mayola's daughter." He caught her chin in his hand. "Ain't that so?" "Yes, sir," said Perline. "I am." "Used to know yo' mama," said Charlie. Perline looked confused for a minute; then she lowered her eyes and giggled like she knew she was supposed to. "Gosh sake, Charlie," I said, "quit horsing around and let's dance." It was hard to get him out of these moods. But I'd managed it more than once, dancing.

Charlie was a good strong leader and the way he danced, one hand firm to my waist, he would take my free hand in his and knuckle it tight against his chest. I could follow him better than I could anybody. Sometimes everybody would stop just to watch us, but the prize that night was going to Pete and Hope, they were shining around with some new steps that made the hoop skirts jounce. Charlie was half drunk, too, and bad on the turns.

"Try to remember what's important about this evening," I said. "You know what Hope and Pete are trying for, don't you?"

"I know I'm always coming home to a lecture," said Charlie and swung me out, spinning. "What a woman for sounding like a wife." He got me back and I couldn't tell if he was mad or not, I guess it was half and half; but right then he almost knocked over one of Hope's floral arrangements, so I said, "Why don't you go upstairs and catch your forty winks? Then you can come down fresh and start over." The music stopped. He blinked, looked tired all of a sudden, and, for a miracle, like a dog that never once chose to hear you, he minded.

I breathed a sigh when I saw him going up the stairs. But now I know I never once mentioned Nelle to him or reminded him right out, him with his head full of oil leases, bourbon, and the road, that she was the real cause of the party. Nelle was somewhere else, off in the back sitting room on a couch, to be exact, swapping family news with Mary Foote, who was her cousin.

Dancing with Charlie like that had put me in a romantic mood, and I fell to remembering the time we had first got serious, down on the coast where one summer we had all rented a fishing schooner. We had come into port at Mobile for more provisions and I had showered and dressed and was standing on deck in some leather sandals that tied around the ankle, a fresh white T-shirt, and some clean navy shorts. I had washed my hair, which was short then, and clustered in dark damp curls at the forehead. I say this about myself because when Charlie was coming on board with a six-pack in either hand, he stopped dead still. It was like it was the first time he'd ever seen me. He actually said that very thing later on after we'd finished with the boat and stayed on an extra day or so with all the crowd, to eat shrimp and gumbo and dance every night. We'd had our flare-ups before, but nothing had ever caught like that one. "I can't forget seeing you on the boat that day," he would say. "Don't be crazy, you'd seen me on that boat every day for a week." "Not like that," he'd rave, "like something fresh from the sea." "A catfish," I said. "Stop it, Eileen," he'd say, and dance me off the floor to the dark outside, and kiss me. "I can't get enough of you," he'd say, and take me in so close I'd get dizzy.

I kept thinking through all this in a warm frame of mind while making the rounds and talking to everybody, and maybe an hour, more or less, passed that way, when I heard a voice from the stairwell (Charlie) say: "God Almighty, if it isn't Nelle," and I turned around and saw all there was to see.

Charlie was fresh from his nap, the red faded from his face and his tie in place (he'd even buzzed off his five-o'clock shadow with Pete's electric razor). He was about five steps up from the bottom of the stairs. And Nelle, just coming back into the living room to join everybody, had on a Chinese-red silk shawl with a fringe. Her hair, so simple and shining, wasn't dark or blond either, just the color of hair, and she had on the plain dove-gray silk dress and the elegant sandals. She was framed in the door. Then I saw Charlie's face, how he was drinking her in, and I remembered the day on the boat.

"God damn, Nelle," said Charlie. He came down the steps and straight to her. "Where you been?"

"Oh, hello, Charlie," said Nelle in her friendly way. "Where have *you* been?"

"Honey, that's not even a question," said Charlie. "The point is, I'm *here*."

Then he fixed them both a drink and led her over to a couch in the far corner of the room. There was a side porch at the Owenses', spacious, with a tile floor—that's where we'd all been dancing. The living room was a little off center to the party. I kept on with my partying, but I had eyes in the back of my head where Charlie was concerned. I knew they were there on the couch and that he was crowding her toward one end. I hoped he was talking to her about Grey. I danced with Grey.

"Why don't you go and break that up?" I said.

"Why don't you?" said Grey.

"Marriage is different," I said.

"She can break it up herself if she wants to," he said.

I'd made a blunder and knew it was too late. Charlie was holding both Nelle's hands, talking over something. I fixed myself a stiff drink. It had begun to rain, quietly, with no advance warning. The couple from Hattiesburg had started doing some kind of talking blues number on the piano. Then we were singing. The couch was empty. Nelle and Charlie weren't there. . . .

It was Grey who came to see me the next afternoon. I was hung over but working anyway. Mr. McGinnis didn't recognize hangovers.

"I'm not asking her anywhere again," said Grey. "I'm through and she's through. I've had it. She kept saying in the car, 'Sure, I did like Charlie Waybridge, we all liked Charlie Waybridge. Maybe I was in love with Charlie Waybridge. But why start it up all over again? Why?' 'Why did you?' I said. 'That's more the question.' 'I never meant to, just there he was, making me feel that way.' 'You won't let me make you feel any way,' I said. 'My foot hurts,' she said, like a little girl. She looked a mess. Mud all over her dress and her hair gone to pieces. She had sprained her ankle. It had swelled up. That big."

"Oh, Lord," I said. "All Pete and Hope wanted was for you all—Look, can't you see Nelle was just drunk? Maybe somebody slugged her drink."

"She didn't have to drink it."

I was hearing Charlie: "All she did was get too much. Hadn't partied anywhere in months. Said she wanted some fresh air. First thing I knew she goes tearing out in the rain and whoops! in those high-heeled shoes—sprawling."

"Charlie and her," Grey went on. Okay, so he was hurt. Was that any reason to hurt me? But on he went. "Her and Charlie, that summer you went away up north, they were dating every night. Then her sister got sick, the one that died? She couldn't go on the coast trip with us."

"You think I don't know all that?" Then I said: "Oh, Grey!" and he left.

Yes, I sat thinking, unable to type anything: it was the summer her sister died and she'd had to stay home. I was facing up to Charlie Waybridge. I didn't want to, but there it was. If Nelle had been standing that day where I had stood, if Nelle had been wearing those sandals, that shirt, those shorts— Why pretend not to know Charlie Waybridge, through and through? What was he really doing on the Townshend property that night?

Pete, led by Hope, refused to believe anything but that

the party had been a big success. "Like old times," said Pete. "What's wrong with new times?" said Hope. In our weakness and disarray, she was moving on in. (Damn Nelle Townshend.) Hope loved the new people; she was working everybody in together. "The thing for you to do about *that* . . ." she was now fond of saying on the phone, taking on problems of every sort.

When Hope heard that Nelle had sprained her ankle and hadn't been seen out in a day or so, she even got Pete one afternoon and went to call. She had telephoned but nobody answered. They walked up the long front walk between the elephant ears and up the front porch steps and rang the old turning bell half a dozen times. Hope had a plate of cake and Pete was carrying a bunch of flowers.

Finally Mrs. Townshend came shuffling to the door. Humpbacked, she had to look way up to see them, at a mole's angle. "Oh, it's you," she said.

"We just came to see Nelle," Hope chirped. "I understand she hurt her ankle at our party. We'd just like to commiserate."

"She's in bed," said Mrs. Townshend; and made no further move, either to open the door or take the flowers. Then she said, "I just wish you all would leave Nelle alone. You're no good for her. You're no good I know of for anybody. She went through all those years with you. She doesn't want you anymore. I'm of the same opinion." Then she leaned over and from an old-fashioned umbrella stand she drew up and out what could only be called a shotgun. "I keep myself prepared," she said. She cautiously lowered the gun into the umbrella stand. Then she looked up once again at them, touching the rims of her little oval glasses. "When I say you all, I mean all of you. You're drinking and you're doing all sorts of things that waste time, and you call that having fun. It's not my business unless you come here and make me say so, but Nelle's too nice to say so. Nelle never would—" She paused a long time, considering in the mildest sort of way. "Nelle can't shoot," she concluded, like this fact had for the first time occurred to her. She closed the door, softly and firmly.

I heard all this from Hope a few days later. Charlie was off again and I was feeling lower than low. This time we hadn't even quarreled. It seemed more serious than that. A total reevaluation. All I could come to was a question: Why doesn't he reassure me? All I could answer was that he must be in love with Nelle. He tried to call her when I wasn't near. He sneaked off to do it, time and again.

Alone, I tried getting drunk to drown out my thoughts, but couldn't, and alone for a day too long, I called up Grey. Grey and I used to date, pretty heavy. "Hell," said Grey, "I'm fed up to here and so are you. Let's blow it." I was tight enough to say yes and we met out at the intersection. I left my car at the shopping-center parking lot. I remember the sway of his Buick Century, turning onto the Interstate. We went up to Jackson.

The world is spinning now and I am spinning along with it. It doesn't stand still anymore to the stillness inside that murmurs to me, I know my love and I belong to my love when all is said and done, down through foreverness and into eternity. No, when I got back I was just part of it all, ordinary, a twenty-eight-year-old attractive married woman with family and friends and a nice house in Tyler, Mississippi. But with nothing absolute.

When I had a drink too many now, I would drive out to the woods and stop the car and walk around among places always known. One day, not even thinking about them, I saw Nelle drive by and this time there was no doubt who was with her—Robin Byers. They were talking. Well, Robin's wife mended the clothes when they were ripped or torn, and she sewed buttons on. Maybe they were going there. I went home.

At some point the phone rang. I had seen to it that it was "out of order" when I went up to Jackson with Grey, but now it was "repaired," so I answered it. It was Nelle.

"Eileen, I guess you heard Mama turned Pete and Hope out the other day. She was just in the mood for telling everybody off." Nelle laughed her clear, pure laugh. You can't have a laugh like that unless you've got a right to it, I thought.

"How's your ankle?" I asked.

"I'm still hobbling around. What I called for, Mama wanted me to tell you something. She said, 'I didn't mean quite everybody. Eileen can still come. You tell her that.' "

Singled out. If she only knew, I thought. I shook when I put down the phone.

But I did go. I climbed up to Nelle's bedroom with Mrs. Townshend toiling behind me, and sat in one of those old rocking chairs near a bay window with oak paneling and cane plant, green and purple, in a window box. I stayed quite a while. Nelle kept her ankle propped up and Mrs. Townshend sat in a tiny chair about the size of a twelve-year-old's, which was about the size she was. They told stories and laughed with that innocence that seemed like all clear things—a spring in the woods, a dogwood bloom, a carpet of pine needles along a sun-dappled road. Like Nelle's ankle, I felt myself getting well. It was a new kind of wellness, hard to describe. It didn't have much to do with Charlie and me.

"Niggers used to come to our church," Mrs. Townshend recalled. "They had benches in the back. I don't know why they quit. Maybe they all died out—the ones we had, I mean."

"Maybe they didn't like the back," said Nelle.

"It was better than nothing at all. The other churches didn't even have that. There was one girl going to have a baby. I was scared she would have it right in the church. Your father said, 'What's wrong with that? Dr. Erskine could deliver it, and we could baptize it on the spot.' "

I saw a picture on one of those little tables they had by the dozen, with the starched linen doilies and the bowed-out legs. It was of two gentlemen, one taller than the other, standing side by side in shirtsleeves and bow ties and each with elastic bands around their upper arms, the kind that used to hold the sleeves to a correct length of cuff. They were smiling in a fine natural way, out of friendship. One must have been Nelle's father, dead so long ago. I asked about the other. "Child," said Mrs. Townshend, "don't you know your own grandfather? He and Sid thought the world of one another." I had a better feeling when I left. Would it last? Could I get it past the elephant ears?

I didn't tell Charlie about going there. Charlie got it from some horse's mouth that Grey and I were up in Jackson that time, and he pushed me off the back steps. An accident, he said; he didn't see me when he came whamming out the door. For a minute I thought I, too, had sprained or broken something, but a skinned knee was all it was. He watched me clean the knee, watched the bandage go on. He wouldn't go out—not to Pete and Hope's, not to Rose and John's, not to anywhere—and the whiskey went down in the bottle.

I dreamed one night of Robin Byers, that I ran into him uptown but didn't see a scar on his face. I followed him, asking, Where is it? What happened? Where's it gone? But he walked straight on, not seeming to hear. But it was no dream that his house caught fire, soon after the cleaning shop opened again. Both Robin and Nelle said it was only lightning struck the back wing and burned out a shed room before Robin could stop the blaze. Robin's daughter got jumped on at school by some other black children who yelled about her daddy being a "Tom." They kept her at home for a while to do her schoolwork there. What's next?

Next for me was going to an old lady's apartment for Mr. McGinnis, so she could sign her will, and on the long steps to her door, running into Robin Byers, fresh from one of his deliveries.

"Robin," I said, at once, out of nowhere, surprising myself, "you got to leave here, Robin. You're tempting fate, every day."

And he, just as quick, replied: "I got to stay here. I got to help Miss Nelle."

Where had it come from, what we said? Mine wasn't a bit like me; I might have been my mother or grandmother talking. Certainly not the fun girl who danced on piers in whirling miniskirts and dove off a fishing boat to reach a beach, swimming, they said, between the fishhooks and the sharks. And Robin's? From a thousand years back, maybe, superior and firm, speaking out of sworn duty, his honored trust. He was standing above me on the steps. It was just at dark, and in the first streetlight I could see the white scar, running riverlike down the flesh, like the mark lightning leaves on a smooth tree. When we passed each other, it was like erasing what we'd said and that we'd ever met.

But one day I am walking in the house and picking up the telephone, only to find Charlie talking on the extension. "Nelle . . . " I hear. "Listen, Nelle. If you really are foolin' around with that black bastard, he's answering to *me.*" And *blam!* goes the phone from her end, loud as any gun of her mother's.

I think we are all hanging on a golden thread, but who has got the other end? Dreaming or awake, I'm praying it will hold us all suspended.

Yes, praying—for the first time in years.

THE SKATER

Haloed in lynx hats that gleamed with softly falling snow, wrapped in fur-lined raincoats, the two Westmount women went gossiping past the Ritz, until somewhere between "Then she said" and "So I wondered" a small figure crossing with the light on Mountain Street passed before them, wearing the red beret. The woman on the right began suddenly, wordlessly, to run after her, around the corner, down the street, half falling on a streak of snow-hidden ice, only to right herself and race ahead, as though silently calling, Oh, wait!

"What's the matter? Sara! You were running!"

She stood panting, smiling at the friend in weak apology. "It's just that I gave Nan's old red beret to the char's daughter. I thought that might be her." A lie. They both stood looking down Mountain Street to where, a block away, the red beret marched steadily on.

Another time Sara dreamed it. It was all the same except that in the dream she caught up, pulled the child around to face her, saw an ugly, coarse young stranger who spit out icicles at her like a mouthful of teeth, while Sara cried, You stole that hat, and raised her hand to strike.

It was like my daughter's beret, exactly, she heard herself

tell some unknown confidante, who would reply, *But that was years ago, fifteen at least.* Then I once followed a boy with his arm in a slate-blue sling exactly like Rob's, the time he broke his arm playing soccer. If only he'd turn and have a face like Rob's. Couldn't that happen, too? And there was Jeff. *Your youngest?* Blond and small once, a tiny, brave boy. In Westmount Park this child I saw—

Forget the confidante, she told herself, lecturing the mirror. They're safe, they're alive, they're married and gone. They just aren't here. You're not making sense.

Then there was summer air, filling the whole strange room. "I wondered so much about you, right from the first. Finding it all out—won't that be great?"

Sara didn't bother to answer. She turned her head, moving it slowly, comfortably, against his shoulder. She, too, had been full of questions. Now, languid, she didn't summon the energy to ask them. It was enough that he was actually there, with his mid-European accent, his learned English, and the one cry brought from a long distance. She rubbed a lock of his black hair between her fingers, like fine cloth.

Day was fading from the windows, slowly, smoothly, like honey being poured carefully. The tree outside the hotel window was at its fullest green. Her eye turned to his watch on the bedside table. It lay beside her own diminutive one with the gold linked bracelet, and the gold shell-shaped earrings, smooth as glass, curved like a snail's back. He liked to stroke them. Time, said the watches. Time.

To go home to Westmount. Stop on the way for groceries. Change to robe and slippers. Cook. Drinks with husband. Dinner. TV. For the man beside her, another world was out there. He picked up the watch and strapped it on.

"Everything seems to run better with us these days," her husband remarked at dinner. "Hard to understand."

"What's hard about it?"

He spooned out veau Marengo. "We used to be always worrying over the children."

"It's change of life," she suggested. "I'm changing for the better."

"You've got used to them being gone. At first that was too much for you."

She finished eating first, and sat with cheek resting on her palm, regarding him, smoking. The images of thirty years were in her memory: his walking through crowds at a station to meet her; her running forward over a lawn to find him; his worried frown at her first flare-ups; his proudly watchful smile above the bow of a wrapped present. She put out her cigarette.

"Something happened today," he said.

He finished his coffee deliberately. Evidently, as though taking a case to court, he was arranging what he had to tell in his mind before he started. He seldom mentioned his cases; he "left the work load at the office." He ate in shirtsleeves and leather house shoes. The dark vest—he was a man who liked vests—cut its usual pattern into the white clarity of his shirt.

"I was just leaving for the day when a young man came in, without an appointment, looking frantic. So I turned back. I saw him."

"And?"

"His problem all spilled out in a hurry. His father had died, but before he died, he had sent him (the son, an only child) a copy of his will. The will left him everything, a considerable estate. But when the funeral was over, another will entirely was produced, and he found himself disinherited. A psychic group is now supposed to get everything, including the house. It seemed to him like a dirty trick, his father jeering at him 'from beyond the grave,' was how he put it. On the other hand, maybe it wasn't the father, but someone else who had forged it."

"Who, for instance?"

"The will the boy had was an informal document—a holograph copy—handwritten. The lawyer who drew up will number two may have been up to some fancy footwork on the date."

"It's not clear which was first?"

"They were dated the same day. That's the odd part. What the boy has is just a photocopy, the original of that one is God knows where. No lockbox has turned it up; the father could be assumed to have destroyed it in favor of will number two. That's certainly what the psychic's lawyer will argue."

"A psychic group. That sounds crazy. Was he?"

"The deceased? Well, he was over seventy, alone in one of those big old mansions way up the mountain. Found dead of a stroke. The boy wasn't living there."

"He's just a young boy?"

"What do I call a boy these days? He may even be thirty. Way behind you and me."

She got up to bring him coffee. Any mention of youth made her wince a little. It was the weak point, bound to surface, in the affair she had stumbled into. Her lover was younger. Safe in the kitchen, she touched the corner of her mouth. Bruised from kissing, it was preciously sore. She took in the coffee.

"Why wasn't the son living there? Was he married?"

"No, he's alone. There had been some hard feeling, some quarreling over his not having work. He assumed that was done with when he got the first will. Anyone would." He folded his napkin on this. He often said that as intelligent as you wanted to be about it, life was never solved. "Haven't you heard of him—old Phil McIvor? He made a pile in mining up in northern Ontario. I won't go snooping around old mansions, but there are certainly matters to explore." He glanced at his watch. It was time for one of his political talk shows on TV.

She felt he had given her a puzzle to play with. "The son might have written the will himself."

"Then why would he have only a Xerox? It was notarized, however. We're checking on that."

She was still clearing the table when the telephone rang. Her husband answered. "Oh," she heard him say, and, "But I make it a strict practice never to see clients at home. Yes, I know I said we would need more time, but I gave you an appointment for next week. I understand. . . . Just a minute." He placed a hand over the receiver. "Sara, by coincidence, it's that boy I was just talking about. He's wandering around alone, got our address, wants to come in for a few minutes. . . ." He paused, looking at her. Such things didn't happen.

"Let him come," she said.

He smiled. "You mean it?"

"Why not?"

They did, of course, both miss the children.

"You're keeping something," her lover said.

"I know," she said, "but it's nothing really to do with me. I mean, it has to do with a case, something legal. A confidence."

"I think it's more than that. You must have legal confidences to burn."

"There's a young man, a client of my husband's, who did a strange thing. He asked to stop in the other night and talk to Ted. He was odd."

"Gay, you mean? Queer?"

She shook her head. "He was intense, troubled. On the raw edge with nerves. Yet in spite of that, or maybe because of it, appealing. It's hard to describe."

He turned her face to his. "He attracts you?"

"Karl, I didn't mean that."

"It's how you make it sound."

"If I meant anything like that, I'd say Ted attracts him. I think he wants to attach Ted in some way."

Attractions . . . attachments. She lived with such thoughts now, enchantment-circled, in a spell. She no longer tracked strange children through streets and parks. That night with Ted and his client, she had sat deciding the boy's real need was not for any will but for caring, making contact. His hair was carrot-red. Long, spiraling scars marked his cheek and neck. She shuddered.

"There should be something gratifying to Ted," she mused, "in such dependence. When he left, he grabbed Ted's hand and squeezed it. I thought he might kneel." She laughed softly, wanting to be done with it, turning her face to Karl's.

"Mysteries are everywhere." He smiled quick kisses against her cheek, into her ear. "Beware the RCMP, watch out for the CIA. Are the KGB as far away as we think?" The kisses found her mouth; the client left her mind completely. It was Karl—Karl Darcas was his name, shortened from something long and difficult, Polish-Hungarian-Jewish—who brought him up again later while buttoning his shirt. "What does he look like?"

"Who?"

"The mysterious client."

"He has bright red hair and thin legs."

"Oh, that's really sinister!" He stroked her hair so that she had to arrange it again. She looked around the room—a neat, plain hotel in the far East End of the city—saw the green leaves of Montreal's short, precious summer. This time, too, they held their midsummer fullness.

The very thought of her husband, Ted Mangham, forming some new attachment had not entered Sara's mind before. "Ted's ex*clu*sively yours, my dear," some old aunt had said, ages ago. But since Karl Darcas had burst in on her, she had been full of new thoughts and feelings; she was like fresh earth turned up in spring. Every entry into the Metro going from West to East seemed a long underwater plunge from which she could shoot upward into new air, hurrying toward further change. Maybe, she thought, Ted needs to get involved. She was smiling at the idea when she came like a rain-washed flower up out of the Metro exit on her way home and noticed the red-haired young man with his back to her, leaning forward to look in a shop window. Her walk's rhythm broke at once; there was a chill moment of hesitance in her heart's pulsing. He's been hired to watch me, she thought. Ted's having me watched. . . .

As a girl, Sara had been fantastic, crystalline. Guarded, reared, schooled, feted, presented. Her marriage to a promising young lawyer had been the natural step to take. Unnaturally—with shock, even—bride and groom had fallen in love. For years they had wanted nothing but an excuse to travel, "to get off by themselves." Family minds were soon to grow impatient. Relatives and friends were enlisted to put a word in; but pregnancy, once, twice, and thrice, laid fears to rest. Ted's shoulder wound up firmly set to the wheel, and passion bloomed more rarely. Sara and Ted, from beautiful and wanton, turned handsome and acceptable. ("Don't talk so much about the children," he warned her. She complied.) Ted-and-Sara: around their Westmount circle it was said like one word. Over Karl's bare shoulder Sara confided to the green leaves: "Ted's forgotten all that silly way we used to be. I haven't. That's the trouble. It's not what people call real trouble, I suppose." "It's real," he corrected, "as trouble goes."

Karl Darcas was one of the bright new TV producers on the national network. In his job he was wary as a badger in the bush, eyes in the back of his head. He had plans for moving on to Toronto; she guessed that from the first, though he never said—playing it close, as Ted would have put it.

She had met him at a large benefit at the Château Champlain, the kick-off party for an annual charity drive. Her Christmas mink, so new she still thrilled to the smell of it, was not even checked at the hotel cloakroom while she cast around for Ted, who had got there ahead of her, and felt someone watching her. Not that she knew him. As his eyes fell away, hers lingered for a moment on his thick black hair, growing low on his forehead but making the face for some reason—the strong nose maybe—not less but more intelligent, as if the brain matter had sent up this rich growth. My fur, his hair, she thought and almost smiled when the eyes whipped back to her own, surprising her. He moved toward her.

"Karl Darcas. Have we met?"

"I don't think so. I'm Sara Mangham."

"Mangham." He drew a paper from his coat pocket. "The chairman . . . just who I was looking for. The CBC is running a spot—"

"Oh, no, not me. It's my husband you want. I'm looking for him, too."

This time the eyes did not waver. "Too bad it wasn't you."

Outside later, in minus-twenty weather, they waited before the hotel, together by coincidence, he for a cab, she for Ted to bring the car around. The mink hood was up. When he stroked the rich fur across her back and shoulders, it seemed the most natural move in the world. Drawn from within, she turned her face up to his. "You look like a northern Madonna," he said. Then, dropping his arm as the car drew up, "Where can I find you?" "I'll let you know," she astonished herself in reply, as the tiny snowflakes of deep cold twinkled between their faces.

Now it was summer, and as he said, they were finding things out. He questioned her—fact after fact, with an outsider's curiosity—but the information he gave her in return was mainly about ideas: Montreal and the French ("Just another ethnic struggle—they think they're different, but they're not"), Canada ("The States will get the whole country someday, piece at a time"), Europe under Communism, writers, political currents, topics she had never heard of, though she had lived through the same global scrambles as he. She thought he might have talked about his childhood or his native landscape, but he didn't; he lived in his mind and his body, not accounting for much in the past. She had to ignore his turtlenecks and scuffed shoes; she'd not the right to change him. He takes me for a sample of Westmount, she thought. But there were plenty of those to choose from, she reflected, and observed the iron-hard line between his brows, the dark cast of beard confined beneath the skin.

"Back to the red-haired man. Did your husband follow up?"

"I guess he's still a client. I'd forgotten about him."

But what she said wasn't true. He had called that very morning. . . .

"I'm watching the house," the strange voice on the phone had said.

"What house do you mean? Who are you?" Blackmail crept another step forward, out of the corners of her mind.

"You know who this is. You were there the night I came. It's my father's house I mean, my house. You know the reason I came up there to you? I had to see what you were like. Once I'd seen you, I knew. Knew I could have hopes. Your husband is not going to listen to me, not in a million years. He thinks I'm a kook. He's a commonsense man. Did you know I've got binoculars? The house is being searched. I'm up above it in the park every afternoon. No, it's not the caretaker. It's one of that stinking psychic group. There's an original copy of the will somewhere—the one I have. Don't you get it? They're after it!" Hysteria. He was tumbling off the edge.

"Leave me out of it. Just don't you bother me."

"I'm alone," the calmed voice said. "I'm alone in the world."

("Before I met you I felt lonely," she had said to Karl Darcas. "The children are gone, you see. I was going mad." "Without you the place is empty as a tomb," her husband told her once when she came back from Barbados. But "alone in the world"—that was another thing.)

"Don't you have a girlfriend?" she asked him.

"When I was young I had a rare bone disease. I was in a cast so long after the transplants the skin atrophied. I had a lot of skin grafts. It's why I look funny. No woman could stand to look at that."

"Some women are forgiving . . . gentle," she said.

"Who wants pity?"

I'll be arguing with him all day, she thought. "Why pick me out? You must know other people."

"It's dangerous to talk. My father was rich. The world is all joined up. I might fall through a trapdoor. I might just disappear. I see you ride the Metro. Women like you take cabs, don't they?"

"I take it shopping. It's quicker."

"Shopping? Over in the East?"

"Fabrics," she groped. "There are places—"

"Now you're explaining."

"Go get a job," she urged. "Something that interests you."

"Things are going on," he said. "Things are going on."

Sara had hung up. . . .

"Your mind is wandering again," her lover said. "Come on, what's it about?"

"Just that boy again," she smiled. "I lied."

"So not forgotten, after all?"

"It's not Ted he's bothering now. It's me."

"Could he be the one who had an estate snatched by a bunch of psychic nuts? I read about it."

"I never said that!" Her astonishment gave her away.

"It was in the paper; you must have seen it. The types seemed to match, that's all. Oh, come on. I'd never say you told me." He lit a cigarette and passed it to her. "Lots of angles there." Meditative, he let his hand wander over her. "Obscure psychic society, old Westmount mansion, people who communicate with departed spirits. The old guy thought his house was loaded with them—tables that walked, rumblings from the attic, creaking doors, groans from the basement, blue outlines of the walking dead."

"You come from Dracula land. Old castles dripping blood. Bats swarming at twilight."

"That's Rumania. Quiet. The old guy decides he's been selected by the dark powers. Either that or he called the psychic bunch and they decided it for him. Their leader's from the States, by the way. Ruttlestern by name. Talks like he's always making a speech: 'Now, my dee-ah, we shall soon have clearly demonstrated . . .' I got this girl to call him up. She recorded what he said—"

"What girl?"

"Somebody on the staff. Nobody special. I was thinking of doing a TV spot newscast on it, really not sufficient for a feature. Just 'City at Six' stuff. A contested will, unusual circumstances . . ."

"If anything led back to Ted. If anything led to you and me—"

"Don't worry. Sara! Don't worry!"

"Then tell me, whatever you do. Promise that, at least."

"On my Westmount honor."

"No. Seriously."

"I promise."

When she emerged into a cloudy summer twilight and went

toward the Metro station she saw the red-haired young man sitting in a coffee bar. She was miles from home; he could only be tracking her. She passed him nonstop, but when the phone rang the next morning, at exactly the same time as before, she knew who it was, beyond a doubt.

"When your father was alive," she asked, "did you sneak up in the attic to sleep?"

"How'd you know that? I haven't even told your husband." Off balance. Well, better him than me.

"The story in the paper. Tales of strange noises."

"He had turned me out. We'd had a quarrel over a job. He said I could come back when I had money of my own. But how to make any? I had to stay somewhere. I'm alone. I told you."

"Your father never suspected, caught you?"

"What *is* all this?"

Sara felt stronger, cleverer than before. "Don't be discouraged," her doctor had told her. "When children leave, women often discover hidden facets of their personality." But, she had wanted to ask, do they see their children coming back, pursue them for the sake of a red beret, a plaid skirt, a hockey helmet, hoping to find those very faces just once more? To say that might well land her in some psychiatrist's appointment book. Instead she had landed in Karl's, who'd lightly said, "The world's a mask. It's my job to strip it off, look at what's underneath, get to the point." This lonely boy's mask now seemed so flimsy it was no more than tissue paper.

"Meet me," she said. "Let's talk."

Before they could meet the next afternoon, there came a spell of cold rain. Wind crashed against leaves that had hardly yet thought of turning. Summer would come back, but not fiercely. In the new chill, she went belted in garbardine, a green satin scarf wound around her head. A cab took her far afield into a neighborhood of delicatessens and shoe repair, souvlaki restaurants and mini-lotto tickets. She entered a walk-down coffee shop way out on Saint-Laurent. The boy was there, knuckled up over a table in a booth, and had scarcely heard her order coffee when he came at her with his question. "How did you know I stayed in the attic?"

"I didn't. I guessed."

"I should have denied it. You caught me off guard. I shouldn't have let on."

She said nothing to comfort him. It's what he gets for intruding on me, she thought.

"You think it was so wrong of me to do that, then not to want it known? If people found out— They'd size me up for a nut, somebody not worth an inheritance."

"Who knows but me? All I did was guess. You went there and lived there unbeknownst to him and he thought the house was haunted. You must have sneaked down at midnight to raid the pantry."

"He was a mile away and snoring. He had a silly old Quebec cook who blabbed to him about missing food, doors ajar, God knows what. Some of it she probably invented."

"She never saw you?"

"You have to understand. The place is as big as Parliament. Whole wings closed off. It's a castle."

"Couldn't you tell him you were there?"

"If you knew how it was! I got thrown out of this job he got me. I had to let the room I was living in, just one room, to a fat Italian woman out of work. She answered the phone for me. Then I'd nowhere to stay. He said I wasn't worth anything. I had to prove myself, get a 'position.' "

"Did you find it?"

He had been facing sideways, looking at a wall painted a faded watery yellow and hung with a dusty bullfight poster. "Who would hire me?" he bleakly asked.

Her own response amazed her. She felt, as if beside her,

the myth presence of her lover, and she put her hand out to him in a moment's tender understanding. "You're desperate, aren't you?"

He was sniveling. Nail biting had made cushions of his finger ends, and it was these that pressed her wrist.

"I thought he cared for me—finally, at last, that he felt something for me. I imagined when I got the will—registered mail—that he'd had a change of heart. That he'd decided to overlook it if I couldn't get the sort of work he had in mind. That out of benevolence, like God on high, he'd finally accepted me. I even went to see him. 'Thank you, thank you. You'll be proud of me yet.' He looked vague. He had these funny blue eyes, never precisely looked at you. 'It was nothing,' he said and walked out in his slippers, looking for a book. Then he dies and I hear about the change of mind like that, on the same day. With nobody to tell me, nobody to explain. Was it a joke he was playing? Was that what he meant by 'It was nothing'—that 'nothing' was what it was? I'll never know."

Sara imagined the half-mocking response Karl might make to the boy: "You can ask the psychic society to look him up." It went against her sympathizing ear.

They were alone in the shop, which was overheating, the door not having opened since she arrived. She slipped out of her raincoat, tucking the skirts up from the trashy floor.

"Don't you think your father may have been more than a little dotty before he died?"

"Suppose he was completely sane, sane as the devil." He turned on her his clear, tear-washed eyes, pale, rimmed with stubby reddish lashes. First God, now the devil. But how could she dream of letting the poor child down?

"Why did you call this morning?"

"I meant to say something. That you aren't riding any Metro to shop for fabrics."

"But now you're not going to say it," she firmly advised.

"Why not?"

"You're not going to throw away the only person who really wants to help."

"Then I won't say it." He was round-eyed with dawning relief.

She took a pen from her bag. "Give me your number."

Karl was away on assignment in Halifax. Sara fought off the impulse to get out the children's toys; she did not even look through their old pictures. She went out instead, in settled weather, and looked at the small hotel, and the tree beside it.

She was learning a lot about Montreal she had never known. She had never eaten in small restaurants where food native to everywhere from Greece to the Argentine was good and spicy, and rich coffees arrived, variously brewed and hot, and unlikely pastries.

"I've joined the psychic society!" She almost burst with laughter at her daring when telling Goss McIvor, the red-headed boy, pulling back a tweed jacket from her shoulders. "It was an idea I had, a good one. They meet down in Old Montreal, a big bare room reached by a creaky doorway off a street that probably keeps icicles straight through July. They've got your father's will there, under glass. It's funny, but I thought they might. It's their founding document. The leader is American and so are some of the members. Americans believe in founding documents."

"It's bound to be a copy, like mine."

"That's the tempting part. It isn't."

"The original."

She nodded. "I heard it from one of the members." She laughed so much she could hardly get it out. "With a copy, the spirits wouldn't respond."

"There's a higher court for you," said Goss. "Well," he added, "steal it."

"I thought of that, but I don't see how I could even try, much less succeed. Anything they could trace to me— There's Ted to consider."

"Then don't get traced."

"I'd be suspected. It might come out in court. What, then?"

"What a situation!" But he couldn't stop seeing the funny side. He had got human by degrees. From bitten nails to sense of humor. Then she saw that a whole area of his left cheek would not smile. Irregular as an island, it was dead. It continued downward past the neck of his shirt.

"You're cured, aren't you? Of that old illness, old trouble?"

"If you call it cured. It didn't kill me."

"It's not that bad, you know—the scar. Not bad enough."

"Enough for what?"

"To make you want to get your own back at the world. To make you think that spying on me was okay."

"But now you're getting something out of it. When else would you get an excuse to join a psychic society?"

"Last night we pulled a long curl of mist in through the window. It refused to take a shape, though."

"That was after it rained. Does your husband wonder where you are?"

"I tell him it's bridge night. He doesn't play."

"I thought lawyers liked bridge. Aren't you ever at home?"

Ted Mangham was cognizant of about fifty percent of his wife's venturings, and the rest he might have drawn up with a fair degree of accuracy if he had cared to do so. But he saw Sara in a perpetual present, a lovely woman seated in his living room, dressed for afternoon, talking with someone he could not at the moment, from the corridor, see, radiating rightness, kindness. How could she really find herself anywhere else for very long? No, not possible, thought Ted. Yet in earlier days, opening the nursery door, he used to discover her down on the floor, crawling about to play with the children and their toys. More than once she was suckling a baby until the very bell announcing guests had made her button up her hostess gown.

"Funny thing," Ted mentioned at dinner. "You know that psychic society I mentioned, the one old Phil McIvor left his house to, or so they claim? Well, there's going to be a TV item on them. The son called to ask me to stop it. They wanted to bring a camera crew inside the house, then move on to that meeting place they have now. Well, we can keep them out of the house. The property is in escrow until probate is over."

"What's his objection?"

"He thinks it's a plot of that bunch of crazies to find the original of the will he has and destroy it. That would leave him without a hope of finding it. Of course, he's more than a little obsessed. Sees threats everywhere."

In quite another setting than Ted had ever seen her, Karl Darcas extracted a document from his briefcase. He handed it to her. "Here it is."

There was an early snowfall. Large flakes drifted through the tree limbs outside.

What she held on her knees was the original of the will the psychic society had had. He had managed to steal it. How? It was like him not to want to fill in many details. She saw a dark-haired ghetto waif in shabby clothes, sent out for bread, moving through smelly streets. She saw a young boy traveling alone through the nights, from contact to contact, scavenging for food in the dark; smuggled by plane out of Poland to Italy, thence to France; handing over money for forged documents; accepting a new name; never looking back. From Montreal, too, he would move on. He had told her so.

She did learn the excuse he gave for getting his hands on the document—the camera would not photograph through glass. With all that wired equipment, a blown fuse was the natural next step. No magic was evoked to repair it as quickly as they might have liked. But there must at least have been a magic Xerox? He didn't explain.

They burned it page by page in a large ashtray. It came to her out of the small flames and oft-struck matches that his risk had been a gift to her. But I'm risking, too, she thought, thinking that if such conniving became known, her own life might well be downgraded forever by people she had always lived among, or, like something useless, thrown out. She walked to the edge of that possibility and took one dizzy look downward. Was even falling as hard as leaving this room? She could join Karl in Toronto, of course (he kept saying it), but she grew silent on the thought, only next to be twisting in a grasp so strong her arms stayed bruised for weeks. "Leave Ted for you?" she heard herself saying. "How could you even want that?" She could never make herself believe him, though she tried.

He sat on the edge of the bed, smoking, staring across the room at her with heavy-lidded eyes. "Your beautiful satin slip," he brooded. "Your shining gold. How to live without them?" "I'm not like that!" was her protest, heartfelt.

She wanted to praise the daring intelligence she had always honored—especially now that he had proved it. But his scorn met her; that quality which went with his defiant shabbiness was raised up before her like a shield. She'd not the strength to strike it down. She murmured something Ted might have said, though scarcely with tear-filled eyes: "I've no method for doing that." For going away with him, was what she meant. "Some women," he said, "have no such problem." What women did he mean? She had picked up bits and pieces of his past: that there was, or once had been, a wife, still in France; that acquaintance in Montreal was not hard to come by. But she had wanted deeper confidence without requesting it; she thought that trust should come and curl up in her lap like a cat. Later, she would think of East European mysteries when she thought of him, and know they had never found a really common language. Nothing in her experience gave him so much as a sentence to start with. Everything he said to describe her life failed to ring true.

"Anyway," he went brutally on, "I did your dirty work for you."

And that, at least, got through.

Still hoarding her bruises like souvenirs, still shaking her head like an old woman to the beat of remembered phrases, she went, some days later, to meet Goss McIvor in a small bar on Crescent Street. They had got into each other's continued stories.

"My mother was a lot younger than my father. We were such pals. She ran off with somebody else, but even then she didn't forget about me. She wanted me with her. He hated her for leaving. He hated me for knowing why. I think that was the source of what he did. I stayed with her a lot."

"Where is she now?"

"Out in B.C. She's happy. I came back for treatments. He could afford them; she couldn't. It was back before Medicare, when it started. It went on and on. All that pain. After the worst of it, I saw that he didn't have anybody with him. So I stayed."

"Then—rejection?"

"You never know how terrible people can be. Until they are."

They wandered into a used bookshop. "You don't ride the Metro anymore," said Goss.

"No need to." She tried to smile but nearly cried, and then confessed, without giving Karl a name or any work, much less telling what he'd done for Goss.

Goss was prompt to summarize. "You didn't really love him or you'd be with him."

"That's easy to say."

They wondered at life, standing among the murder mysteries.

"It's that silly will case again," Ted told her. "It's just taken a new turn. The will those psychic people have is only a photocopy, too. I could have sworn the original was what they had, because their lawyer was so cocksure. They claim the TV crew took it. But the man who did the show has gone to work in Toronto."

"Can't they contact him?"

"My understanding is that they did. I think they've no proof of theft or they'd bring charges. Of course, that would attract a 'bad press,' as it's called."

"But what did the TV man say?"

"He said they were crazy."

"There's scarcely news in that," Sara said. "Everybody knows they are."

He smiled. "They burn rose petals to invite the departed to speak. Once they sacrificed a budgerigar." He paused. His level stare was on her. "Yet you joined yourself for a while."

She jumped, then braced. There might be more to come. "Yes . . . I was curious. I've been depressed at times over the children. There was Nan—I kept remembering her as a child. And Rob, too."

"Let's not forget Jeff," he added.

"Oh, not for a minute!"

Over his shoulder, she glimpsed her face in a mirror. The eyes seemed lambent, too bright, larger than they should be, like some oversize moth in a sort of fantasy film her sons had once loved to see. If Ted pushed her . . .

"Nobody could have known who I was. I wore plain clothes, just an old skirt and sweater. I went only twice, that was all. It was dark, and people just sat on folding chairs in the background. They passed out leaflets with funny chants on them.

I didn't sign anything," she hastened on; "or give my real name."

"A girl from our office we sent to check out the scene—she saw you there."

His paper was there to read and he read it, until she said, "You remember when that red-haired boy first showed up that night? I could have sworn he was trying to attach himself to you, in some serious way."

"I thought that, too. I think he was after a father, one way or another. "Maybe a mother was what he found."

She made no answer, but sat twisting her rings. "I suppose he'll win the case now."

"It certainly begins to look that way."

She watched him resettle his glasses, which he habitually removed to speak, and resume reading the paper. His gestures had come through the years to be where he himself lived and was defined; she could in no way imagine her own life without them to give it shape, like a mold she was poured into.

No need to tell him (was there?) that she had gone with Goss McIvor that very afternoon actually to see the father's house. It was part of the western mountain's outline, as though along with the mountain it had been discovered there—a grand castellated bulk, rising violet-colored through the snow-dimmed afternoon. "In mining camps, half freezing," he said, "my father dreamed of such a place. Then, just when he hit it big, this came on the market." It had belonged to some railroad owners, a prodigiously wealthy family whose descendants had sold out and gone to Nassau to live out their lives escaping taxes.

"I've got a job," said Goss. "He might like me better now." Leaving, she kissed him on the scarred cheek.

No way or reason to tell Ted either that coming home, down steep streets past tall houses, she remembered her own childhood and the skating rinks of Westmount. Calls from somewhere near came to her, and the click and urgent rush of blades. Had that old McIvor man once looked down from some turret window and seen the skaters racing, twirling, and spinning through slants of snow? She felt herself among them still, a red scarf flying. As dark came on, how far outward she would go, inscribing wide parabolas, while known voices grew distant through the dark.